Praise for Eyes

… considerable dramatic momentum … handled with sympathetic intelligence. It's good.

Kirkus

Eyes is chiefly a novel about conscience, and Miss Burroway has used a melodramatic situation so skilfully that despite the taut, hour-by-hour narrative, her intelligence demands that one stops to think beyond the stock responses to race, human dignity and the morality of protest.

Times Literary Supplement

A cool look at a day in the life of a group of citizens … in the American South. Although most of the characters are threatened by sickness or problems of conscience this is not an apocalyptic Southern novel but and ironic and affectionate study of people facing trouble.

Observer

EYES

EYES

by

JANET BURROWAY

with an introductory interview by
ROSELLEN BROWN

SANDNESS

MICHAEL WALMER
2025

Eyes first published 1966
© Janet Burroway 1966

Introductory interview first published in this edition
© Rosellen Brown 2025

This edition published 2025 by

Michael Walmer
Little Pradies
13a Melby
Sandness
Shetland ZE2 9PL

ISBN 978-1-7638700-3-1 paperback

ERRATUM

This edition has been created utilising a previous edition; thus errors
have been reproduced. On page 178, line 9, for *Chatanooga*,
please read *Chattanooga*.

SEEING EYES

a conversation between Rosellen Brown and Janet Burroway

RB: One of the remarkable things about *Eyes*, published in 1966, is that many of its themes — or, more loosely, preoccupations — have come full circle and feel incredibly current. So, to begin, will you talk a bit about how you came to this story, what there was about it that caught your attention in the mid-60s and induced you to learn enough about eyes to present a coherent story built around them as metaphor and actuality.

JB: I'm aware of two ideas that came together in the (if you can call it that) plot of *Eyes.* The first is that when I was at Cambridge (England) in the late fifties, I had a boyfriend whose father was director of a major psychiatric hospital in the U.K. The father was a great talker, and one of the things he talked about was having practiced (and possibly invented) "sensory deprivation" as a means of breaking enemy POWs in the Second World War. It involved confining them in small, dark, smooth and sound-proof cells where, deprived of sensation, they would become disoriented and compliant. After the war he developed a method of using sensory deprivation as a curative technique for psychiatric patients, especially the senile depressed.

The information had long ago been declassified. It was not surprising that he was going to lecture on it to a London colloquy of medical students. What none of us expected — though yellow journalism was alive and well in England — was that a reporter would cover the speech and declare the method torture. There was a furor, such that Churchill stood up in the House of Commons and denied that there had ever been, or would ever be, such an outrage practiced in England (it had taken place on the Continent, of course), essentially calling the doctor a liar. The press pounced, the doctor's house was besieged with reporters and paparazzi — and he had a heart attack and died.

I knew there was a more complicated story here than had appeared in the press, but also that I would not use it in such a way as to betray its source. But how to find some other "experiment" that would carry the same potential shock-value?

I write fast but I think very slowly. By the time I had decided that eyes, and cutting on eyes, would carry the necessary weight, I was married, out of graduate school, and spending the summer of 1961 with my new husband in New Orleans. He had been a passionate member of an N.O. jazz band in his native Ghent, and our summer was spent almost entirely at Preservation Hall (which was then just beginning to be famous), listening, holding the basket, and getting to know the musicians. Charlie Love had had a stroke, and my husband took cornet lessons from him to encourage his fingering, while Lizzie Love taught me to make gumbo and Inola Barnes to make red beans. I am basically unmusical, and this summer's intensity was a revolution, made more intense by the consciousness that a rift with my parents over their racism was overdue, and perhaps imminent.

By the time these two experiences fused and I actually sat down to write the book, I had a baby and we were living in Ghent, where I did my research in Flemish with a very patient optician and a lot of models and diagrams; and made up an un-named impressionistic city for my setting, because there was no way, there, then, to research what I didn't know or had forgotten about New Orleans.

RB: It's very satisfying to see that you were able to use so much of an actual story so directly, transforming it via your (typically) finely wrought details and your (also typically) elegant sentences. The eyes are, of course, both real and metaphoric. Oedipus and the wise Tiresius come to mind: How can the eye surgeon fail to see what he was party to? How can Jadeen, who thinks she's wise to and exempt from the racism all around her, not recognize her own profound blind spot? Do you attribute these responses, so recognizable and familiar, to the unique personalities of these characters or would you hold their place in the worlds they've grown up in (Jadeen as a "nice Southern girl" and Dr. Rugg as an arrogantly self-assured, widely respected pillar of the community) responsible? Or would you opt for all the above?

JB: Let me start by saying — what I'm sure you know but readers sometimes need to be reminded — that the idea for the novel came out of those experiences, but it is not autobiographical: neither Rugg's nor Jadeen's experience was my own. In fact the desire to get inside their viewpoints, because they were not mine, was a source of my thinking about eyes. I was interested in looking, not at eyes but through them, at what they see and what they don't.

You ask: how can they? But such blind spots are inevitable in us. I know less and less what a "unique personality" is, apart from the contexts that form us. Jadeen believes she has severed herself from her mother's kind of sweet-talking "reasonable" racism, but when her mother seems to be attacked, it is her mother, not her own beliefs, that she defends. I believe Jadeen's relationship to the music and the musicians is personal and profound, but when she feels sexually threatened, she falls back on the hypersexualization of the woman dancer and confronts Hilary in the ugly language of her Southern upbringing. Where Rugg is concerned, I think it's not so much his social standing that deforms his vision, as that his crucial experience was as a military man (Honor, Brotherhood; Americans are the good guys), together with his medical status (medical research is good per se). If you told him his experimentation is dehumanizing in the same way as the Nazis', he would think you stupid.

(Later: coincidentally, I have run across some notes in a journal from the early 1960s when I was working out the scheme of *Eyes* and still thinking it might be a play, "north-northwest of realism". I was pretty clear on the character of Angus Rugg ("conceited, vaunting, warm, dedicated") but less certain who Jadeen was ("perhaps a Southerner, if this could be managed…"). In both instances I was less subtle than in the novel itself about the moral implications of each character's blind spots: re Rugg: "That's exactly the same thing that happened at Auschwitz!" About Jadeen, "shares a lot of the prejudices…but does care a lot about teaching, and recognizes that the book is illogical and badly argued propaganda.")

I said *Eyes* is not autobiographical, but in one sobering way it has become so. At least five of my nine novels have to do with race, and though they differ by century, continent, and theme (and indeed by race — the characters being Black, Mexican, Chinese), in each case a central white heroine confronts a racial issue or disparity and learns through it. For many years I have said that I "didn't choose race as a topic; it chose me," and in many ways that is true. It is only now that I have an enhanced vocabulary to discuss such issues (critical race theory, microaggression, white ally, systemic racism) that I see I have written these stories from a position of white privilege. I don't think I could have done otherwise; I grew up white, in a Christian family blind to its own hypocrisy; and everyone has the right to write from their own experience. I also, firmly, believe that the attempt to see through another's eyes and experience is empathic, and that imagining each other is a crucial global need. Still: beware thinking you (I) have uprooted all the forms of bigotry of which a human being is capable. All we can do, re racism, is try again and fail better.

RB: Maeve is a very believable "stay-at-home mom" — a phrase that didn't exist back then — a woman perennially defined by her devoted domesticity. (If there's anything to be said about the number of years separating the anticipated baby from its older brother Hilary, who will be more like an uncle, I missed it.)

She is sane, committed to the trivia that make households run, but because she doesn't need to be center stage, only a supportive foil for her abstracted husband, I worry about her after the final curtain. She will manage because she is good sense personified, but I'm sorry she will have to raise that child alone.

Did you feel the need for a character who sort of holds down the center, not ideological, not preoccupied by the tensions and conflicts "out there" while she soothes and protects her two men, this husband who may or may not get home for lunch but will expect it if he does, and her intense and self-satisfied son? Like so many women, she gently critiques but ultimately humors them.

To put it another way, do you see Maeve as an exemplar (and a positive one) of your forceful maxim – which we'll come back to – that "Thoughts are complex. Actions are not."? She does have a rich sense of irony and of the troubles of the world beyond her front porch, but she feels it, you might say, locally. I love the rhythm of this prose as well as its attentiveness to scale: "Never sufficient receptacles for the refuse. Never enough bags for the garbage, tenements for the poor, hospital beds for the sick, marriages for the children, sea for the sewage." Her satisfaction appears to come from the small daily duties – attending to the garbage, the laundry, to stocking the larder – because for all her inner qualms, she who "had no talent and no fondness for housework" sees herself contentedly and without bitterness in service to the men who truly matter in the world.

JB: The reason the phrase "stay-at-home mom" didn't exist back then is that staying at home was the norm. Only exceptions need identifying. Then — remember? — the exceptions that were identified were called "career gals," or, if academics, probably "bluestockings," and were expected to stay single and childless. A woman with both children and a job was rare, probably either very poor or rich-and-famous. Maeve grew up poor in Ireland (we know, because the profusion of choices in a supermarket dazzles her, and makes her remember what "shopping" meant as a child: cabbage, potatoes and tobacco). At some point she immigrated and she has done very well for herself by marrying a prominent and well-off doctor — better than she could have imagined as a child. Once married, she would not have thought of taking another job, if that had ever attracted her. At the same time, she has two prescient thoughts. One is that there isn't room for all the garbage we humans create (to tell you the truth, I think it was a tiny bit prescient of me to think that on the page in 1964), and the other is that being a stay-at-home wife is never quite satisfying. All she has to look forward to is Angus' arrival, and it always slightly disappoints. Let's say Maeve was born in the nineteen-twenties, and had Hilary in her early twenties. He is now in his early twenties, so she's mid-forties, and the late pregnancy is obviously a surprise. Pre-pill, that happened to a lot of women who used rhythm method, or self-protective abstinence or, in the fifties, a diaphragm. They went for a long time without a child, and so got careless and were surprised late. Maeve is happy about the baby, though, and Angus's death will be devastating.

But. I think she'll grieve — and survive. The Irish poor are great survivors. I think the baby will be a burden and a solace, and that she'll just get on with it until she's okay. Also, once it gets around that Angus was hectored by the press, sympathy will turn her way. She has already, very deliberately, figured out that she might need the bourgeois Dodie. Others will flock to help.

I hadn't thought of her as holding down the center. Nor had I thought of Maeve as an example of the maxim that action is simple. But she is. The others are all involved in personal drama of some sort or other. Maeve acts for others, always getting-on-with-it, and in that sense I guess, yes, she holds down the center. (I've talked myself round to it.)

Jadeen is in that way more fragile, less resolute, than Maeve, and I hope Angus's death won't derail her plans to leave. She will certainly stay a while, to help and comfort both Hilary and Maeve, and then I hope and think she'll hew to her decision that she needs to find a different milieu.

RB: Janet, I've loved hearing your thoughts about your book, and now, to close the circle, I have one final question: Though it was not your first novel, you wrote *Eyes* quite early in what has turned out to be a very impressive career. So – inevitably – I'd like to know what, so many years and so many books later, *Eyes* looks like to you now, no pun intended. I don't need to tell you that many writers are embarrassed by their early work, though perhaps just as many are impressed — even surprised — at the energy and the daring they demonstrated when they were still in what I think we can call their literary, and even their lived, innocence. Do you have some late words about these early words?

JB: Isn't it a long apprenticeship we wind our way through? Well, maybe not you — you seem to have been born full flower as a poet and then a novelist. But for me, the first novel, *Descend Again*, offered me a tentative sense that I might get inside another mind and find a way to write from there. The second, *The Dancer from the Dance*, was written from a single viewpoint — that of a minor American diplomat in Paris, a "sixty-year-old smiling public man." What possessed me?! I had a sort of Jamesian vocabulary for him, but what being in one mind mainly taught me was that it was very difficult to know what was going on anywhere but in that mind! — and that it might be hiding a few things from me too.

But *Eyes* was the first time I deliberately chose multiple viewpoints and assigned chapters to each, so that the reader ultimately knows more about both the characters and the events than any one of those characters does — a form I eventually called "cumulative omniscience." Of course, many writers were and are writing in this format; it might be fair to call it the dominant way of telling a story in the twenty-first century, a replacement for and a displacement of the omniscient author of the nineteenth century. Perhaps it is even a (snarky) response to the postmodern notion that "the author does not exist."

Are there moments in these books that embarrass me? Sure. Any moments that surprise me with their energy? Sure. In my experience every new book is the first book; it requires you to seek and stretch in new, never expected, directions. And when the final MS is sent off to the presses, it pretty much ceases to exist. As Stephen Graham Jones says, "Now? Now it's time to write the next one." There are exceptions, but I think most authors have some experience of this sort. So, when and if you go back to read an early publication later, you yearn to cut this paragraph, revise that image — and at the same time, you think: wasn't I smart back then, compared to the Googling oaf I am now? Where *Eyes* is concerned, I think what strikes me is that it was in these pages that my characters and I began to see the force of irony — from the verbal irony of Mama Lilly's telling Rugg, "You have a good heart," to the essential irony of Jadeen's liberal choice: "They receded from her as palpably as people outside the window of a starting train…all the Negroes she had ever known to call by name."

It's usual for me to see an intriguing situation, start writing about it, and let the characters tell me where they're going. *Eyes* was the only novel I've written for which there was an outline in advance. I needed that kind of organizing because my baby was ten months old as I began my daily writing stint. So, every morning I put the playpen beside the desk and stacked the desk with toys. When he began to fuss I would coo at him and hand down another toy. On good days he would accept each with delight, and would also fall asleep and give me a blissful hour of real concentration. But of course sometimes the toys were of no interest, and he would demand my full attention. I was pretty much isolated from other mothers in those Ghentian days, which made me fall back on myself and the writing, and perhaps that was a sort of blessing, but it was hard. Now I feel myself to be part of a vast international — what would you call it? — a Fecundity of Women, a Bounty of Women? — a PerSisterhood determined not to trade one kind of creativity for another.

ROSELLEN BROWN and JANET BURROWAY

Chicago, January 2022.

For WALTER

Thanks are due to
Dr. F. Van Hees, optic surgeon,
and Mr. P. Michiels, optometrist,
both of Ghent

Noon, Rugg

Elvira—that was his mother—had at least enjoyed her dying. You could hardly say she had taken her time about it, she had been forty-two. But she'd begun early then, really at eighteen, with a bubbly syncopated cough and what they called an ulcer until nervous stomachs were invented, which it had then been until it really did turn into an ulcer around aught five.

Beginning here, at the upper, older end of Boulevard Admiral McPhay, you could see down balconies and bowing eucalypti to where the tower of the *Morning Watch* marked city centre at Alvarado. But McPhay went farther and you could see no farther, because this town had grown up higgledy-piggledy around people's claims and squattings; nobody came and laid the streets out with the deliberate notion of a city. You could not see it bend and follow the department stores into Charleroi (Charleyroy) Place, bend again past warehouses and filling stations and then, still called a boulevard though it was not and still called McPhay though it had changed character twice already, bend once more through stately ex-residences now housing Elks and Baptists to end snub against the front of Medical Centre. A damnsight too far to walk in this kind of weather. Dr. Rugg stopped by his car, shifted his limp jacket to the other arm and got the keys out. But then he made the mistake of touching the door handle. He jerked his big hand back and waited for the molten pain to flush through him, both ways from his stomach, it seemed, instead of from his hand. He was surprised to find that he wasn't numb and he thought, I'm surprised that I feel anything because *I don't feel anything*. He stared at a pattern of wrought maple leaves over his head; all the ironwork recalled faraway flora, not a banana leaf or a moonflower anywhere: and he found that it, his feeling nothing, did not wake any feeling in him either. All the same he didn't think he could bear that hotbox, so he put the keys back in his pocket. The balconies and the trees always seemed more complicated when it was sweltering like this. The heat came off them in eddies and undulations, so that although they were perfectly real they, funny, seemed to belong to a mirage. He started walking.

She had spent a good deal of time on her feet and doing what mothers did, no doubt about that, but when anybody said "your mother" and very often when anybody just said "mother", there she was in his mind, sitting half up in a fourposter with one hand extended to show how very little skin and how very many rings there were on it, saying, "Oh, splendid, it's so *sweet* of you to ask, really much better this morning," in such a way that you wouldn't have laid odds on her honesty but, courageous, my! Good thing she could afford real lace, there wouldn't have been half the show without it. Hanging everywhere, the limp kind, like tree moss; off her wrist, her collarbone, festoons of it around the posts, spilling down the bed sides. What a good time she'd had! And then, bless her, when it really *was* the end and she really *was* in pain, she'd got so used to acting that way that she just kept on with it and turned out courageous after all, slipped off one morning without any fuss, looking like an etching called *Among The Angels* or *The Final Peace*, and very pleased about it too.

Whereas he, who had had a full half-century to look it

square in the eye, or come to terms with it, or make his peace with it, or whatever you *did* with death. . . .

One of the slow southern girls approached him, elegant in bare-armed black, her eyes loitering along at her own pace. But as she came even with him her glance jerked raggedly around from one ear to his chin, his nose, the other ear. People were always doing that. They stumbled over his face as over cornered objects in a hall. She smiled distinctly and disappeared beyond his shoulder. Rugg held his pace and his eyes front for the space of a quarter-block before he turned and looked after her, and found her doing the same. Regret overtook and overwhelmed him. The image of Jadeen Spatch turned slippery over in his mind like soap and, very slowly wearing thin like soap, gave way to the figure of Maeve in the one pink linen thing she had bought to wear. Eight months big now, carrying it all in front because her frame was narrow, carrying it careful and clumsy because it was late to be pregnant and she felt fragile; or rather did not feel it if you could believe her, felt dull and slow, but looked as if she felt it, her pied face balanced breathless on her long neck and the blue of her eyes deeper, than it was, not darker but deeper as if the colour came from farther down in her, closer to the core. For the first time it struck him that he might die before his son was born.

At that he felt something, something in general that made him stop and set one shoulder against a phone booth on the sidewalk; but also something in particular, a sharp pain about two inches long and no bigger around than a piano wire, set diagonally left to right in the space just above his balls and which could have nothing whatsoever to do with his disease. None the less it was what he was most aware of, and in the middle of feeling queasy, with his legs doing something

11

they'd made up on their own, irritation made room for itself and ballooned up in him, that he should be set upon by an irrelevant pain. My God, I am sick and tired of my mind, he thought. All he wanted was to concentrate with clarity and depth upon the one particular fact, and so make it his own in a way that had so far escaped him. But the closest he could come to a cosmic reflection was the interjection Jesus Christ!, which he repeated swiftly several times beneath his breath.

His glaring reflection in the phone-booth glass was cut across the nose by a red slat. Below, his breath made a fuzzy circle looking rather like his mouth felt inside. Also below, his nose made for the pane like a glass-cutter, while above his eyebrows lunged in threatening it with a severe tickle. At one time or another his "forehead", "brow", "jaw" and "features" had all been described in the newspapers as "craggy". Whenever he particularly wanted to needle his son (the older one, the old one, not the unborn one) about The Quality of Journalism in This Country Today, he claimed, quite untruly, that he had never been described by any other adjective. He also made up sentences from fictive newspaper articles that began, "Craggy-pored Dr. Rugg," or, "Dr. Rugg's craggy left armpit," or especially, "Dr. Rugg flexed his craggy pelvis as he . . .".

Dr. Rugg put his craggy right hand in his pocket and fumbled among the anomalous contents of it for his cigarettes. There was a hole in the pocket that he told himself to remind himself to ask Maeve to sew up before he lost something out of it that he didn't know was in there. Then he thought that perhaps this would not be worth the trouble, and he saw that, whether or not he assimilated it—It—which he very likely never would, he would never again regard acquisition or repair without reference to it. He lit a cigarette and drew

12

deeply, smoking out his reflection as he exhaled. This made him feel definitely better, his legs shaped up and so on, and this in turn made him wonder if he weren't sinning. He threw the cigarette in the dry gutter and stepped inside the phone booth. He'd only come a couple of blocks from Trippin's, but aside from the waste of energy (nor ever again expend energy without reference to it) he did not want to *see* Trippin again, just to talk to him.

"Good afternoon, Drs. Trippin and Harfield. . . ." The receptionist had a downy cotton-candy kind of voice, suggesting that she was a northerner putting the southern accent on. She drawled out the "Harfeeeeld" *just* interrogatively enough to make it clear that she was not saying good afternoon to Drs. Trippin and Harfield. In person, this girl had a pair of perpetually parted moist lips and a simply tremendous bosom. Rugg thought she had probably taken up nursing for the same reason that girls wear men's shirts at the beach: the uniform looked as if it ought to look so severe, while actually providing a perfectly blinding expanse on the slope. He also thought the girl was Trippin's mistress, but where he had got this idea, or anything more on-the-surface-of-it unlikely he could not imagine.

"Dr. Rugg." The sudden, arresting image of Trippin and Miss Wetmouth discussing his cardiograph in bed, made Rugg's voice go husky. "There's something I forgot to ask Trippin. Can you put me on to him?" he asked, noticing that he kept just enough emotion out of his voice to make it clear that he was trying to keep the emotion out of his voice. He found his perceptions sharpened, especially with regard to himself, as if he were several per cent more alive than usual, and he found this, contradictorily enough, unpleasant.

"Of course, Dr. Ruuugg. I'll put you raight through." Her

13

voice was caressing, comforting, but whether more than usual, or more of the latter than the former he could not judge.

"Dr. Trippin here."

There were little patches of moisture around his finger-tips on the receiver. Across the street somebody was shaking a mop over the edge of a balcony. He could see the motes all this way, which reared violently upward when two boys on a motor-cycle came screaming through them, braked and made a U-turn around the tree island at a perfect forty-five-degree angle.

"Trippin here. Hello? Dr. Trippin here."

There was something so very damn pompous about that "here" that the irritation balloon blew up again and exploded the words out of his larynx in a way he had not at all intended.

"Rugg *here*. Can I SMOKE?"

"Beg pardon? Is that Gus?"

"I want to know whether I'm allowed to smoke. Cigarettes."

"No," Trippin said primly. "I wouldn't if I were you." Rugg could hear in his tone the way the muscles had tightened on either side of his thin mouth, drawing it straight out. He could also hear a regular metallic tapping that was probably Trippin's pencil going up and down on an X-ray frame.

"If you were me," Rugg blared at him, "there's a lot that wouldn't get done that I'm going to do. You can take your *reasonable precautions* and . . ." he added a string of therapeutic obscenities from which, however, he went directly to feeling foolish without any intermediate stage of feeling purged.

"That", Trippin said, "is why I didn't mention it. Now suppose you explain, that being the case, why you telephoned."

Trippin never said anything in his life—no, not "good to

see you," not "it could happen anytime"—without managing
to make it sound as if he were having the last word on something or other. Those mouth muscles must be the most fully
developed Trippin had. Yet he would never, never tell Trippin what an ass he was; not because he had any particular
scruple about doing so, but because the opportunity simply
wouldn't arise. If he lived to be ninety the opportunity would
not arise, but he hadn't known that he would live to realize
that he would not live to tell Trippin what an ass he was. All
the things he would never do and never know began climbing
into the phone booth with him: tell Trippin what an ass he
was, whether Trippin had discussed his cardiograph in bed
with Miss Bigtitties, whether he and de Sevres had been
justified in their experiments at Reuzarne in '44, put his palm
on the melon-plump bottom of his born son's fiancée, where
de Sevres's reports were now, make a functioning artificial
eye, see the Negroes inherit the earth, receive the Nobel prize,
whatever made his son go into the newspaper racket, ride a
motor-cycle at forty-five degrees. . . .

"Look, Trippin, don't you think I could have elephantiasis
or leprosy? What I mean, something a ways out of the common run?" It was very crowded in the phone booth now and
he thought he would have to get out soon.

"Heart failure, Gus," Trippin said in his reasonable we're-
adults-now way. "Ordinary heart failure."

This flat refusal of Trippin's (and Trippin was his best
friend) to go along with him in his choice of attitude towards
what was, after all, his own even if he had not made it his own
yet; this finally seemed more than he could stand. He couldn't
stand it in the same way he couldn't stand it when some
woman's club woman asked him in the question-answer
period, "Doctor, do you feel that it is right to interfere with

15

Nature like this?" and he answered, "Madame, Nature is a bitch," and she answered, "But I mean do you feel that it's right to interfere with the natural *processes?*" But this time, as a result of his not being able to stand it, a most astonishing thing happened. He began to cry. His throat swelled rapidly up until there was no passage left in it leading to his lungs or his stomach, and all the excess fluid that had been swilling around in his head found egress at his eyes.

"I'm sorry, Rugg," Trippin said, but he had said that before, and it would have been nice if he'd been sorry enough to go along with him. Since there was no hole left leading from his lungs, Rugg just pushed what air he happened to have in his nose out in a snort and hung up. He catapulted out of the phone booth and was able to breathe a little. Then he went over to the gutter and, bending carefully, retrieved his still-smoking butt.

When he straightened up he found himself being regarded aghast by a heavily powdered middle-aged-to-elderly female face rising out of an incredible volume of ochre fichu. The woman looked a little bit familiar and very much like one of the club presidents or a University trustee.

To her credit—Rugg gave her credit—she did not avert her eyes when he noticed her, and this more or less challenged him. He meticulously inspected the butt, brushed off a few specks of dust, and inhaled. The woman lowered her head, snorting bull-like, and charged on her way.

The cigarette, or the encounter, had opened his throat up again, and he walked on finishing the cigarette very quickly, in long pulls. His eyes still felt a bit juicy, but no more than his armpits or the insides of his thighs. My craggy eyeballs are sweating, he thought. He thought that something mildly defiant was in order, like placing a five-year magazine sub-

16

scription or a bet on the 1970 Series. Or buying, acquiring, something fine and useless.

He passed Cordoba Chambers, a Med School annex where he was to give a (not yet written) guest lecture that evening and, although it was 12.45 and his appointments began at one, crossed at the corner and continued away from Boulevard Admiral McPhay. The atmosphere immediately changed. All those hanging vines and peek-a-boo courtyards fell from sight. The three and four tiers of balcony dropped so abruptly down to one-skimpy-storied clapboard houses that it looked like the construction rubbish behind a movie-set façade. A little farther on the houses were propped up on cement pyramids and had steps tumbling out of them that might equally well have been kindling piles. Anything you moved in the shadow of one of these houses would dislodge a half-dozen sleek black cockroaches—everybody was black here but only the cockroaches ate well—who would then scuttle into the shin-high clumps of grass between the broken paving stones. But you could tell it was still the middle of the city because every other house had a shutter like a roll-top desk and a bin out in front offering used thrillers or cheap vegetables, and because there were a few white women with white gloves on going through from somewhere on their way to somewhere else. This was referred to as the "new section" of the "old quarter" because the houses occasionally fell down and, that way, nearly all of them had been put back up again at one time or another since the turn of the century. Two blocks away on McPhay the price of land was figured by the square foot, but as long as the Negroes continued to live here, the land would continue to be cheap enough for them to do so. A great number of them of both sexes and all ages and conditions of health were sitting on the kindling steps with great

B   17 stolidity as if they realized that this was the only power they had in the city and they were going to be sure nobody stole it out from under them.

Rugg stopped before a construction that was not so much a house as the roof-papering of the space between two houses, this one not on stilts so that it seemed to have slipped down and got wedged between two that were, and that had a blackboard out in front on which was written in some glutinous substance not chalk, "Mama Lilys Junk Antiquities and Voo-doo". ("Don't you mean Antiques?" he had asked her once, and she answered serenely, "I spells it the French way.") The tarpaper was partly obscured by a collection of hubcaps, bed springs, and mended overalls hanging from nails in the one window frame. On a stool at the side sat an ancient very tall man with an impressive street-length conical yellow beard and a clump of mucus dried into the matching moustache. In spite of the heat he had a wear-burnished army topcoat over his undershirt. A mouse-coloured fedora, empty, lay brim-up at his feet. He nodded at Rugg and touched one rheumy eye in salute.

"Why aren't you on the Boulevard?" Rugg asked. "You can't make anything here, surely."

"Yes, you come to Mama Lily's," the old man said, advising or approving, one; adding in a stage whisper thin with mystery, "She got something special for you she been saving." The old man coughed into a hard handkerchief.

"Shouldn't you go down to the Boulevard?" Rugg shouted. He always spoke to Negroes at double volume and although he knew that this was sin number one for a liberal he had long ago given up trying to break the habit; he settled for blaming it on his mother. "You'll never make anything here."

"Yas," the old man smiled and nodded stubbornly, al-

18

though he was not deaf and Rugg had made enough noise to bring Mama Lily out—a short, compact high yellow whose face was a relief map of some very good country for fighting in, and who wore a pair of men's slippers caved in at the heel and a weight of glass and wooden beads from which her neck was constantly ducking away.

"Doctor Rugg," she said, managing to put a great deal of satisfaction into these words without making them entirely affirmative; and he replied, "Mizz Caffey," because he categorically and ostentatiously refused to call by his or her chosen nickname anyone who would not call him "Gus", which Mama Lily could not, although she once or twice tried "Doc", which he rudely discouraged.

"It's no use his sitting here, is it?" Rugg asked her, and Mama Lily, drawing him into the cave of her junk and antiquities, all the rafters hung with second-hand garments worth less than the hangers they were suspended from, like a strike meeting of listless and despairing ghosts, answered exactly as the old man had done, "You come to Mama Lily's. I been saving you something special."

She touched Rugg with excitement and when she let go of him performed some swift and complicated motion of protection vaguely, but only vaguely, like crossing herself. The house, store, shed, whatever it was, led back for a distance that would not have been suspected from outside, opening by a bead-curtained doorway on to another room that was the living-quarters, and from which came the noise of a number of voices and even more silences—infant and female, all of them, because Mama Lily's family was of that kind that perpetuates itself in every slum, all the women showing a remarkable fecundity without any of them ever producing, or at any rate holding, a wage earner.

19

"How about a cup of coffee?" he asked.

"Yas, you sit right there I'll get you a nice cup of coffee and then I'll show you what I been saving you up, it's something."

She poured him a cup from a pot on a hot-ring and brought it to him steaming. It was mostly chicory, harsh and pungent. The taste was as specific to Mama Lily's as the sight of the jars on the shelf above him, ominously labelled "Moccasin" and "Swamproot", but mixed in with the most domestic sort of kitchen bowl (Mama Lily would sell either the bowl or the concoction) and garden tool and broken appliance. He tasted the chicory-cum-coffee and looked at these shelves as if he had been away from them for a number of years, and he learned—he was learning these things one at a time—that his brief stop at Trippin's had produced a great artificial distance, loss of time, in him, so that when he got there he would probably look at his office door and his dog-eared green desk-blotter in the same way.

"You wait now. I'm going to turn my back, don't you give me the evil eye." She laughed a high nervous neighing without humour, not really even quite turning her back because (while Rugg would not even bother to argue with her about the efficacy of voodoo, except as commerce) Mama Lily regarded eye surgery with a disapproving awe, and tried to get him to admit that he had like her sold his soul to Mumbo-Jumbo.

So without quite turning her back she unearthed from a rummage pile a perfectly cubical wooden box with a metal catch, the box nearly a foot on all sides and the catch foolishly small. He supposed that whatever it was must be good because she never expressed confidence beforehand. She only set things out before him, watching his face and puzzled, even perhaps to the point of thinking it part of his evil profession

20

and being frightened by it, when his fancy hit on a piece of pocked metal that had no use or a hand-worn section of ship's rail. And her puzzlement was reasonable because he didn't know any more than she did about antiques and didn't care to. He only liked, liked well enough to want to own, apart from any desire that Mama Lily should meet the mortgage payments, certain particular old pieces of brass or oak or even sometimes (like the *naïf* ship-in-a-bottle made by a real clipper captain; like the barometer face and crystal, the works lost but the FAIR and STORMY delicately etched in blue ink by what must have been a female hand) glass and paper.

"You wait now." She had a sense of presentation, Mama Lily; something Rugg had himself and valued highly. He would like to have set her loose in the display windows of Mallaby and Stern around Christmas time; that would be something. Of the materials at hand she chose a low packing-case, which she set at his feet, a woman's royal purple cotton skirt, which she spread over the case, and an ivory tatted shawl, which she spread over that. Then she placed the box on top of all of it and produced!—like that, because it was the sort of box with hinged sides that fall when the lid is lifted, and she had clearly practised the motion with which to do this—a multi-layered moulded plastic model of the human eye, such as every medical school commissary stocks by the gross and an earlier, plaster of Paris, edition of which had been the first toy that his son Hilary had been allowed to destroy. Rugg laughed immoderately. He had a moment's vision of himself bringing and presenting with flourishes a burnt-out lightbulb that he would want her to believe was a crystal ball. He closed his mouth on the laugh and opened it again to tell her about this so she could enjoy it too, and saw that Mama Lily was watching him with incredulous dismay.

Distrust. He leaned forward and flipped aside the conjunctiva, cornea, iris, until he came to a split layer in the model and said, "There, you see, no use. Frigging lens is half gone. Why, Mizz Caffey, this eye can't even *see.*"

He laughed again, to be accompanied, but was not. Mama Lily closed the sides of the box—lifting them one by one; this had not been practiced—set it back on the shelf among the rummage and walked to the door.

"Well, woman, show me what else you've got," he said, but already knowing without having got over being surprised by it that she would answer, as she did, sadly and yet coldly, "That's all, Dr. Rugg. That's all I had to show you."

He went outside since she seemed determined on it, looking for a moment at her beads that blinked in the sun and trying to figure out how to make it right until the old man, who must have been thinking about it in the meantime until he thought this up, said, "Well, you see, I don't go up to the Boulevard no more because it seem like Mizz Abbeville don't want me hanging around there no more." He cleared his throat and spat into the handkerchief.

"Shit," Rugg said. "You can always sit on Gypsy's corner, can't you? What have you taken in today?"

"Nothing, Dr. Rugg." This was offered by a woman in the doorway, who had followed them from the inner doorway, and who looked as Mama Lily must have looked ten years ago although, being Mama Lily's second youngest daughter, she was at least thirty-five years younger. "He can't make it down to the Boulevard no more."

"Cigarette?" the old man asked him anxiously.

Rugg took the handkerchief away and glared at the blood in it, then shoved it back into the old man's lap. The yellow eyes went guiltily down into the yellow beard. Rugg fumbled

22

for his cigarettes again, gave one to the man, took one himself and lit them both.

"I'm not supposed to either," he admitted, feeling strange in his stomach when he said this because he seemed to have heard so many other people say it though he could not think who. The daughter laughed and she and Mama Lily, Mama Lily still distant, polite, shook their heads at the pack Rugg held out to them.

"As far as I'm concerned," Rugg said, more than ever loudly and from-a-lectern because he did not know how to right things, "that beard of yours is a civic institution and the tourists have got to pay for it."

"Yessir," the daughter said patiently, "but he can't make it down there no more."

"Don't you know anybody with a car?" he asked the old man. The daughter answered for him again: Mama Lily had disassociated herself from them by the mere drawing of her neck back against the beads, and the old man watched his cigarette, not to miss a moment of it.

"We know anybody all right, but you see they don't like it so much Grappap going down there. It don't look right."

"Look right hell," Rugg said. "If you've got a car you can afford to look right. It don't look right the kids going hungry either." (This also he did, and knew he did—used the wrong form of the verb and an occasional double negative. But after an hour with McFadden at the Centre he came away with a Scottish accent, so you couldn't prove anything by that.) "Wait a minute. Hasn't one of the kids around here got a toy wagon? It's your Emile, isn't it?"

Grappap concentrated on his smoke absolutely. The woman dropped her eyes and, for lack of anything better to do, dusted the door jamb with her blue crepe skirt.

23

"Sold the wagon," Mama Lily finally, resentfully, said, resenting not the selling of the wagon but the saying of it. Her saying it started something, put a possibility between them that would end one way or another and, one way or another, change the relationship between them, so that she resented saying it for all of them, Rugg too.

But it was too late now. "You could buy it back," Rugg suggested and the daughter, still dusting the door jamb while Grappap coughed into his crusted handkerchief and Mama Lily turned the force of her coldness on her now, sullenly nodded. Her nod did not mean that she could in fact buy it back—which the question had not meant either—but that if Rugg gave her the money it would be possible to do so and that if he did she would (not necessarily buy the wagon back but) accept it.

Mama Lily plainly was not going to jump in with something that he could appear to find a bargain now, and if she did not and he gave them the money he would have cut himself off from the one tone with which he knew how to jump the central fact between them: I am rich-distinguished-and-white and you are poor-obscure-and-black. If he bought them a wagon to get Grappap down to McPhay where he could beg efficiently, then he could no longer say, fahchrissake go down to McPhay. He even only gave Grappap one cigarette at a time so that when he said quit smoking Grappap would not feel obliged to do so. He knew that they needed his money more than his friendship but he overrode the argument on that hand with the other one, that some rich distinguished white bastard had got to try it this way. He would simply have returned the nod and changed the subject (which would have altered the relationship in another, but less damaging, way, because he would then in effect have refused them) if

24

today had not been today. He had not begun to realize how many things, not simply acquisition and repair but also lending, giving, selling and relinquishing, would no longer be carried on without reference to It. He now had just even odds for outlasting the old man, and if he did not then the former friendship of his cadaver would not be worth a worm in comparison to a child's toy wagon that could get Grappap into the tourist area, especially if the child who no longer owned the wagon got rickets. So it was a form of "what's the use" that made him finally decide to say, "How much would you need?"

"Ten dollars," the daughter promptly replied, which was an obvious out-and-out lie, carelessly obvious, and just went to show you how quickly things deteriorated when they started to deteriorate. Rugg took both five-dollar bills out of his wallet.

"Well I guess I'll have the eye," he said to Mama Lily, who went in and got it and came back and handed it to him without a word while he, in order to show her that he absolved her of responsibility for it, handed the two bills not to her but to her daughter.

"Might as well be hung for a goat as a quid," he said, and, although the daughter did not get the joke, she got both that he had made a joke and the general significance of it, blushing blue as she accepted the bills and rolled them up to stick between her breasts.

"Many thanks, Mistah Rugg," she said with heavy gratitude, and Rugg thought, that's right, that's *just*: demoted by one medical degree for a ten-dollar fee, because Mistah is the man who gives them money. There were six cigarettes left in the flattened pack and, feeling surly, Rugg threw it down in the old man's lap.

25

"Two a day, not more, you hear?" he said, out of habit, and with a sinking in the pit of his stomach—which seemed to have been sinking about every ten minutes for the last hour without ever coming up again—he saw the old man raise his eyes in that phony innocence that is the major component of black gratitude to white condescension and solemnly form the words, which came out sounding like a pop song chorus, "Too-ah-day."

Then Mama Lily as he departed roused herself and said, would have to have said or she would never have got and held a reputation for being a voodoo queen, because such reputations are based on the knack of saying the right thing without knowing what you mean by it; said, "You've got a good heart, Dr. Rugg," repeating as he started and backed off nodding denial and good-bye, stumbling over—what?—nothing, his trouser cuffs flapping around his ankles, "You've got a good heart, Dr. Rugg," repeating until he was half-way down the street and out of earshot carrying the box with the eye in it, "A good heart, Dr. Rugg, a good heart."

One o'clock, Jadeen

Jadeen took one whole side of her hair between thumb and forefinger and, pulling hard, anchored it behind her ear with a severely plain tortoiseshell clip. It immediately, before she had finished doing the same to the other side, began straining upward and releasing, spring-like, a multitude of hairs in every shade of cadmium, copper, wheat, brass and flax, the hairs working individually but tending to one deep-looped wave toward the eyebrow on each side. She frowned very insincerely at the failure of the effect and caught the back into a rubber band, around and over which the curls snapped like a flytrap, concealing it entirely. The warning bell sounded for the end of second lunch. Over her shoulder Cassie Van Looy, her face oddly disfigured by the blisters in the Teachers' Room mirror, closed her James Bond and stretched.

"There they are, these kids, do you want to know what they're doing right now, right this minute? Five minutes left and there they are, just straining. The ones in class, naturally. *Strain*ing. Books half shut ready to snap, crouching in their desks ready to spring. I swear these kids."

"Rhranph." Miss Trevelyan, shifting her bulk on a straw-bottom chair and poking at the pins around her hairpiece, made an agreeing, not agreeable, noise. "They never change." Jadeen thought that Miss Trevelyan was probably in a position to know.

"Here they are, their books half closed, ready to snap." Cassie Van Looy demonstrated with her James Bond. "They just *can't wait*. Have you ever seen anything else from them? I swear, I think we ought to get rid of that warning bell, I really do."

"Wouldn't help," opined Miss Trevelyan.

I'm just beautiful, Jadeen thought with an upward rush of astonished emotion, just *beautiful*. I could be in a movie about pioneers, I'd wear a pink gingham dress and a sunbonnet; or in an ad for menthol cigarettes. She saw herself on the green stream-bank, the sunlight falling equally on the waterfall and her varicoloured golden hair, her lips slightly parted, smiling up at . . . at Hilary, very red with sunburn and absolutely exasperated, saying, "*Men*thol *ciga*rettes! Jadeen, your *val*ues!"

Jadeen giggled. Cassie Van Looy, still leaning forward with her thighs half-lifted from her chair in demonstration of the crouching now going on in the classrooms, glanced gratitude at her and amplified her theme, "No, and some of them start getting fidgets waiting for the warning bell. Some of them don't think class is good for anything except getting out of, I swear."

Miss Trevelyan laughed with the most tremendous pleasure at this, as if it was the sort of thing that just made her day, saying, ". . . except getting out of", under her breath and letting the gelatinous stuff of her upper arms quiver and wobble in a way that none of those now-crouching kids had ever seen. Jadeen ran a puff over her face; she thought it was just as well never to be too rosy. She pulled her belt up a notch—that made it twenty-one inches, as you could just about guess from the side—thought better of it and let it out two.

"They simply aren't at *all* interested in education," Cassie Van Looy concluded, delighted at her success with Miss Trevelyan and gathering up her things in a crisp, but also gawky,

28

way. Jadeen had seen teachers' pets gather their things up that way, taking hold of everything with great concentration so as to keep their nerves from showing.

"Why should they?" Jadeen said, and would have been sorry immediately if Cassie's face had fallen, but it didn't; she and Miss Trevelyan exchanged a look, so she continued, "What's it ever done for them?"

She went to her pigeon-hole over the coat-rack and took out an attendance sheet, her notebook, a paper-back edition of *Hamlet* and a turquoise-blue hard-cover called *Tripping to Arcady*. The name of her position, English: Rotating Supply, was typed neatly below the Geraldine Spatch on her pigeon-hole. This designation meant that, although permanently employed, she had no permanent classes, but merely filled whatever vacancy might occur or (more often) took over the study halls so that the regular teachers could get papers corrected. When Dr. Rugg heard the name of her job he said, "You *what*?" and lay down on the divan and kicked with laughter. Hilary said, "He's putting it on," but none the less by the end all of them were roaring. So that at first she had been nervous about introducing herself in the Teachers' Room (and especially in the cafeteria where, although they sat at different tables, the men teachers did come and did occasionally exchange a remark with the women across the aisle); but it had been a month now and nobody had seemed to see anything obscene or even mildly amusing about her being a rotating supply. They must be used to it.

"Well, back to the old 10B grind," Cassie Van Looy said, while Miss Trevelyan's chuckling went on behind.

Lastly, she took down an offset-printed book with a plastic spiral spine; not large, but printed on a slick kind of paper that made it astonishingly heavy. The title was in block letters

29

like a newspaper headline: *RACE AND THE HUMAN RACE.* Jadeen weighed the book in her hand for a moment and put it back on the shelf. Then she took it down again, weighed it again and slipped it into the pile of books on her arm.

"Bye, Jadeen," Cassie Van Looy said. "Who are you this afternoon?"

"I don't know. Have to ask The Bridge. Bye-bye."

She stepped into the corridor and was enveloped by the sour, exciting smell of adolescent sweat, which never—as if the smell itself respected the boundary, knew its place—crossed the threshold into Teachers' Room. As a student she had not been conscious of the smell until, in the locker room at State, she had recognized it and been struck momentarily dumb with fear of, longing for, this grey-green corridor now before her with its receding double row of photographs. She paused and half-back-stepped, the way children ritually do before a sidewalk crack that has been designated as poison, beside one of the narrow frames. It was the fifth from last (meaning, among other things, that those who had entered as freshmen the fall after she got out had just got out last spring) group picture of the senior Parnassus Club. So quickly that no one would have thought she had time to focus, she picked out first her name from a dense line of four-point type and then her face, shoulders, torso, in the middle row that was seated on the auditorium steps.

The girl in the picture was distinctly fat. Chubby, adults had said, but Jadeen had known all along, fat. Squinting in the sun, her eyes were almost hidden by the globular supremacy of her cheeks, her forehead was shortened by a tumble of too-enthusiastic curls, her thick tubular body encased in an unfortunate pinafore with ruffles over the shoulders.

30

There was almost no chance whatsoever that any student would ever recognize her or—even less likely—take the trouble to count out the names and discover that this was she. But just to be sure, she always left the Teachers' Room before the last bell sounded and offered her glance to the photograph before the homerooms spilled into the halls, finding it necessary to perform this minimal rite for a reason that never remained the same two days in a row: to remind herself that things could be worse, to keep her from getting conceited, to buck her spirits, to admonish her frivolity, to teach her gratitude, to prove that will mattered. Sometimes she looked at Hilary two frames later too, but this was not *necessary*. Hilary looked exactly the same now as he did in the picture and not even any older: long, the homely hungry kind that made you say "basketball" to yourself even if you knew him.

The bell did ring now, and the homeroom doors opened in one great sucking sound, followed by the confusion of an infantry in flight, book backs reporting against each other and the floor like scattered rifle fire. The intense wet heat of the afternoon came suddenly alive, and attached itself to every released young body, every fact, every thought. A huddle of freshman girls over a photograph brushed by her, and it was hot. Reed Nelson, six inches taller than she already, passed with a salute vaguely insolent, and it was hot. At the end of the corridor the tight, square form of the tragically misnamed Bridget Honeywell gained her office and disappeared, and it was hot.

Jadeen had lost the fat late, had been babyskinned, dimpled and wretched until one day in the summer immediately following the photograph she had done something so insignificant that she could not now recall it; refused dessert, or got diarrhoea, or slept through breakfast. And almost immediately

31

afterward she had discovered that her breasts were more prominent, and that she could feel her hip bones poking up when she lay on her bed, and that first the red kid belt and then the brown suede one would go up one notch farther, and then another, and then they were too big altogether and had to be shortened at the shoe repair. It was time for her to lose it, she would have lost it anyway. But for two summer months, going to the pool every day until somebody would notice (they were incredibly slow) she lived on boiled greens and soup beef, not because these were necessarily the least caloric available dishes but because, by the stern inversion of an engaged will, whatever was hardest *must* be most effective.

No one, least of all herself, had ever suspected what bones she had been hiding. In another country, or at another time, she might have "come out" then, and lived as a beauty for the rest of her life. Here, now, she had lived for at least five years in the conviction of her universal undesirability, under the perpetual reminder of her mother's disappointment. So she didn't entirely recover. She still had the pleasure of surprise when someone called her pretty, but it made her shy, which made her preen, which made her less so. Any contemporary of approximately the same endowments, but who had had them since she was twelve, could wither her in seven seconds flat.

She knocked on Miss Honeywell's door and went in. The Bridge (this nickname had no significance except its general solidity; it was passed from class to class with such clandestine glee that Jadeen had been absolutely stunned to find the teachers used it too) was running a pencil down the afternoon schedule. She had taken off her grey linen jacket and was standing in a pale blue shirt, looking a little less masculine than usual for that, but Jadeen knew that she would put the jacket on again before going off to her next class. She wondered what—it wasn't the school board, it wasn't propriety, it certainly wasn't the weather—seemed to Bridget Honeywell to require that she wear all of a linen suit on the twenty-first day of September.

"Afternoon, Miss Honeywell. Shall I take library north again this afternoon?"

"Ah, Jadeen." The Bridge looked up and gave her glasses a short, sharp push upward, the gesture continuing directly back into a smoothing of her shingled grey hair. A man's gesture. "No, I've got something difficult for you this afternoon."

Jadeen's heart began to pound violently, foolishly, and she sat on the edge of a chair and put her books on her knee, trying to look attentive and nothing else.

"Mrs. Kitchener wasn't feeling well and I sent her home. I'll have to ask you to take her classes this afternoon and probably tomorrow."

"Yes'm," Jadeen said.

"I'm not happy having such short notice for you because her fifth period is non-zam and they have to be sat on *hard*. If you're afraid of it I'll trade you with Mr. Luce, but I'd rather do as little fussing around as possible." Non-zam was the designation used for students who didn't intend to take the college entrance examination. It was automatically assumed that they had no use for school at this level either, and on the whole they kept this reputation up.

"What are they reading?" Jadeen asked.

"Yes, well, that's the worst of it. *Hamlet*. They hate it, of course."

The violence inside gradually dwindled and diminished until both her breathing and her heartbeats were going on again without her having to listen to them; reminding her of

C   33 the time she had stolen her mother's silver filigree bracelet and worn it to somebody's birthday party and then got it back into the drawer in the pound roll of drugstore cotton without getting caught. Drained, stricken with relief.

"No, I'm not afraid of them," Jadeen said to Miss Honeywell. "I'll have to take them sometime. It might as well be today."

"Good." The Bridge nodded a man's brief ducking nod. "Just let them know no nonsense right from the beginning and you won't have any trouble."

Jadeen let her head fall slightly in ambiguous assent.

"You've started off fine, Jadeen. I'm pleased. For your mother's sake as well as yours."

Jadeen tried to make her face express the same matter-of-fact, impersonal pleasure with which The Bridge delivered this compliment. Cassie Van Looy said the trick with The Bridge was to say everything as if you were reading it out of the twelfth grade Civics text. Jadeen got a little tired of Cassie Van Looy's brand of humour, but there was something in that.

"From what I gather, you're quite a favourite already. The only thing that I think you might be on your guard against is a certain . . . informality in your teaching. It diminishes your authority, Jadeen, and you are a bit young still to be able to afford it."

"I haven't had any disciplinary trouble, Miss Honeywell."

"I know, Jadeen. But, for instance, none of us is terribly excited about *Evangeline* any more, but if you tell students that it is 'boring', you see, you imply a criticism of the teacher who . . ."

"I didn't say *Evangeline* was boring, Miss Honeywell, I said Longfellow's use of the dactylic pentameter was boring,

34

in comparison with Whitman's, who was describing the same kind of forest. I . . ."

"It amounts to the same thing, doesn't it, Jadeen. Well, never mind, it doesn't matter"—slicing abruptly into Jadeen's unvoiced protest and taking her schedule up again in evident dismissal. The Bridge was a more flexible department head than most; Jadeen wouldn't have wanted to trade with any of the others she sat with in Teachers' Room; but she had an unanswerable way of deciding "it doesn't matter" of any proposal or protest she planned to veto.

"It wouldn't do to be late to a non-zam," she said now.

Jadeen said "Yes'm" and "Thank you" and opened the door to the corridor.

"Oh, yes, by the way, Jadeen. Mr. Alsuth will be going to state convention day after tomorrow, so you'll have his 11A's for the rest of the week. They're on the *Human Race* thing. It'd be well to look it over."

Jadeen took two full beats with her hand on the knob before she turned and closed the door. Like modern dance class at State: one, two, turn and lunge. She felt very calm and she suddenly remembered that, although she was terrified all the time she spent in a car with Hilary driving, the one time they had really had an accident, when she could see it coming and there was no way out or around and no alternative and no doubt, she had suddenly been not frightened any longer, just thinking to herself: well, yes, I thought so, we're in for it now. And really if you thought about it clearly all they'd got was a shake-up and a scolding from the cop and the bill for a new door.

She came back and sat down on the same chair and put her books back on her knee the same way and looked at The Bridge who was smiling her touchingly noncommittal smile.

She said, "Miss Honeywell, I", (and already the worst of it was over, because that was the main audacity, the main conceit, that: I, Geraldine Spatch, twenty-two years old fresh out of Teachers' State College with three and a half weeks' teaching to my credit) "don't feel that I can", (don't feel that I can was better than won't even if it wasn't as forceful because you had to make it clear that you'd thought about it, that you weren't just being impudent) "teach out of *Race and the Human Race*."

"Don't you, Jadeen?" Miss Honeywell said.

"Because my . . ." Rehearsing it, she had allowed for a number of alternatives, later in the argument, to Miss Honeywell's probable answers. But not here, at the very beginning, where she always said, "Why, Jadeen, why not?" in an astonished voice, so that now after the "because my" Jadeen paused, hearing that calm "don't you" with a kind of impatient incredulity, stumbling over the next word, "subject", which came out "subjub", and feeling the colour rise up her neck until finally she realized that she could go on anyway, that it would be the logical next thing to explain why, even if she wasn't asked. But the colour was already there, all the way up to the roots of the hair that was straining harder than ever now against the tortoise-shell clips, and she wished she could say "overs" the way they used to playing jackstones and go back to when she closed the door. But the most she could backtrack was three words, or two words and a tongue-slip, so she took a breath, holding on to her books hard, and said, "Because my subject is English."

Then The Bridge was supposed to say, "But this book is in English," or "I don't understand what that has to do with it," or, if she were very quick, "*Hamlet* concerns a political situation in Denmark, and you don't refuse to teach that."

36

But she said nothing, nothing at all, pushed her glasses up again without going on to smooth her hair and looked pleasant, even amiable. The alternative arguments went through Jadeen's mind like the headlines in lightbulbs that went around the tower of the *Morning Watch*, and she tried to catch on to one of them and tack a transition on the front of it that would take the place of the responses The Bridge wasn't making. So far all that had been said was, "I don't feel that I can teach out of *Race and the Human Race*: Don't you, Jadeen: Because my subjub: Because my subject is English," and this had begun so long ago that it was not enough words to fill the space between. They hung there foolishly like one pair of stockings on a fifty-foot tenement clothes-line.

"It isn't a matter of the subject matter at all," Jadeen said, which lost some force because Miss Honeywell hadn't suggested that it was. And she had never noticed those two "matters" in the same sentence before.

She put that out of her mind, she put a stop to that. She took hold of her kneecap with one wet palm and plunged, knowing from debate club that if she got sufficient impetus it would be all right; it was thought out in advance, it would just go of itself if she threw herself hard enough into it, over the first dangerous ditch. A finger-nail caught her stocking and a run tickled slowly down the inside of her calf all the way to her ankle.

"As an English teacher I wouldn't feel justified in rejecting the book on grounds of its subject matter, or even on moral grounds," Jadeen said. "I may not approve of the viewpoints of Lord Chesterfield or the Marquis de Sade, but if I were told to use them as models of composition I couldn't very well refuse. But as an English teacher I must be able to use my

37

texts as just that, models in composition, examples of skill or brilliance with the language. I must be able to say, this is an ingenious use of the ballad form, this is a well-constructed essay, this is how good writers use persuasion, inversion, simile, the colon. Because otherwise I *am* teaching the subject matter, and then Emerson belongs to botany and Hamlet to history and all that properly belongs to my subject are poems about poetry and books about books."

"Is the text *so* bad, Jadeen?" Miss Honeywell asked, and that was the first thing, the only thing she did that was accounted for in the rehearsals.

Because to that Jadeen could say, with the least hesitation of any part of it, "Yes, Miss Honeywell, I'm sorry but I think it's so bad. It starts being bad before you even open it, because the word "Race" in the title seems to mean the races, the idea of race, and when you begin to read you discover that it doesn't mean that at all, it means the black race, not therefore as opposed to the white race but as opposed to the human race. And you needn't go any farther than page ten to find a very impressive statistical survey proving that the ratio of intelligence quotients in a large city is directly proportional to pallor. Which not only ignores the economic, social and socio-logical factors, but by its own very specifically stated logic must prove that all geniuses are albinos and all albinos are geniuses." (Like the Nazis, she always burst out at this point when she went over it by herself, but she held that in because she had said no subject matter. It was a different kind of flush on her forehead now. She could go on now indefinitely if she was challenged.)

"So that if I take that text into a classroom, I'll have nothing to say about it honest to myself or to my students except, 'This book is inadequately researched, speciously

38

argued and not worth your trouble.' Which is worse than saying that *Evangeline* is boring, isn't it, Miss Honeywell?"

Miss Honeywell sighed, the sort of sigh that says it's a very hot day to take the children to the zoo. "Is that the reason, Jadeen?" she only asked.

"It's . . . sufficient reason," Jadeen said, confused again now at the disparity between the bristling, disciplinary Miss Honeywell in her mind and the tired, not quite attentive Miss Honeywell across from her, pushing at her glasses once more and taking up the telephone. She dialed one-five, Teachers' Room.

"Hello, who is that speaking please? Oh, Lauralee, Bridget. Is there anybody from English there? Yes, good, will you ask her to step down to 142 and sit on Kitchener's non-zams until Jadeen Spatch gets there? Tell her I'm sorry to cut her free period, but I don't think it will be more than five minutes. She can have somebody recite to-be-or-not-to-be. Many thanks."

The Bridge hung up and set her forearms on the desk with a sweeping motion like clearing a space.

"Now, Jadeen, let me give you a simple outline," she said quietly. "Your family has lived in this city since before it was a city and before it was a town and before it was a corporated village. As the last member of that family you have been under pressure since you were a child to maintain and perpetuate its traditions. This pressure you very naturally and healthily rebel against. Hilary Rugg's grandparents came here not fifty years ago from the north, brought the north with them and planted it around them. Hilary Rugg went north to university and found very amenable certain ideas not compatible with southern reality. You fell in love with Hilary Rugg and simultaneously found one of several—one of several,

39

Jadeen—possible issues on which to base your rebellion. Having quarrelled with your mother you now find yourself committed, in a way that leaves you with grave misgivings, to the attitudes of your fiancé. And that is why you do not want to teach out of *Race and the Human Race*."

The Bridge stopped and she was evidently waiting for an answer. Jadeen was stunned by the accuracy and insight of what she said and also by its blind blundering misunderstanding. Hilary said you could do that in a newspaper with plain facts, that proportionally fewer people died on the highway on the Fourth of July than on an ordinary week-end; but she had never come up so flat against it before. You would think Mommy was one of the plantation family-proud, or a Catholic at least. The Bridge had known Mommy so many years, and did she still think it was the Ruggs' ancestry she would mind, instead of their atheism? She could see what Mommy would do if you told her that her daughter had turned nigger-lover to thwart her: flutter her finger-tips across her mouth in a sweet self-effacing wounded Lutheran way and say, "Me? Why, *me*?" And then Hilary. Suppose she said, Miss Honeywell, but Hilary wants me to teach the book. Then all the rest that Miss Honeywell said would seem to be wrong too when really what troubled Jadeen most was that it was all right and it was Hilary that seemed wrong, out of character, *slanted* to take that side. The Bridge was waiting in a confident mild way as if the issue was obviously solved now.

"All right," Jadeen said. "Those are the reasons I'm not willing to teach it. If I were willing to teach it there would be other reasons."

The Bridge made the same space-clearing gesture as before.

"If you go into Mr. Alsuth's class day after tomorrow and refuse to take the prescribed text with you, the School Board will ask for your resignation. If you refuse to give it they will fire you. If you look for a job within a radius of three hundred miles the particulars of your dismissal will be forwarded and you will not be hired. If you go to the extreme north you will find a job and you may even enjoy the brief notoriety of a heroine. But you will have to leave Hilary Rugg behind, or else Hilary Rugg will have to go north where his ideas are neither new nor needed. In the one case you damage your life and his, in the other you end by damaging the cause you set out to support."

She's been expecting it, Jadeen thought with the most incredulous, ascending astonishment. She's been rehearsing it like I have, but she's better at it, she's had more practice. It isn't fair, she's had years of practice.

"I want you to think it over carefully, Jadeen. You're a good teacher and you do good here. This is not the way to do it. Let me urge you to talk it over with your mother, and to present the issues unglossed to Hilary. I'll expect to have your answer at the same time tomorrow. You may go."

Jadeen obediently got up and went once more to the door, stopping once more with her hand on the knob when The Bridge's voice came after her, altered in tenor, dulled and with the sting gone out of it like a bell you put your hand on.

"Ida Bergen is with the class, Jadeen. Would you like me to keep her on today? You can go get some coffee and come back for sixth period."

"No thank you, thank you very much, Miss Honeywell," Jadeen said. "I guess in the meantime I'll just teach all the classes I've got to teach."

But she went back to a mirror first, not Teachers' Room this time but to the girls', which would be empty now. She took out the rubber band and the clips and brushed the ends

41

of her hair out and up just below the ears, a flip-do like the girls themselves were wearing. She carried a spare stocking—that was something they did teach you at State—and she put that on, did her eyes and took the belt up both notches. It was the red kid belt that she used to wear when this john was her rightful john and it—the belt—was six inches longer before she had it fixed at the shoe repair. She picked up her books and went out.

She could hear 142 from several rooms away along the corridor, a noise that was no louder than talking but the intensity of quiet shouts, and that was peculiar not to the non-zams but to the state of being substitute-teachered at. Ida Bergen's voice was above it and among it, maintaining supremacy only by the higher degree of hysteria it dared show.

"Did Mrs. Kitchener assign you this passage or did she not? Did she or did she not? Have you looked at it? Have you *seen* it?"

Ida Bergen was leaning over—leaning literally over because the boy's long legs dumped on their heels prevented her standing any nearer him—a pitted blond-fuzzed face wearing an expression of the most stunning, exemplary vacuity. Jadeen recognized the boy as Stuart Bordle; it did no harm to know a name. And the girl behind, aiming a trustful look at Ida Bergen and drawing a pencil eraser sinuously back and forth between Stuart's shoulder blades, that was Mary Ellen Church. Two names. Good.

"Thank you very much, Miss Bergen," Jadeen said. "I'll take over now."

Ida Bergen straightened up, from the thighs because she was corsetted all that way—God, on a day like this, Jadeen thought—and gave Jadeen as she passed a look that was all eyelid, meaning, "*Nothing* can be done. I wish you luck but I doubt it." As soon as Miss Bergen was out of sight, not waiting for her to be out of earshot, began the low, accurate imitations of dog-growling and the whistling that was done with the teeth and tongue but fantastically behind closed lips, which Jadeen always got in a new class but which were ruder and more insolent here because—Jadeen knew no one who had ever questioned this cause and effect relationship—because these boys were not going to go to college.

She sat down at the desk and made a leisurely inventory of the contents of Mrs. Kitchener's middle drawer. Then she inspected the attendance report that Ida Bergen had made out, not ignoring but rather looking with a grave deliberate blankness when Stuart Bordle slid down farther in his seat and set his toes against the corner of the desk.

Jadeen was a good teacher. She knew that, and she knew what her quality as a teacher was, well enough to call that quality by its right name and to acknowledge that it was an odd one for her profession. It was called The Dumb Blond. It depended for its success—she knew this too, and it bothered her a little—on the general dishonesty of other teachers. It consisted in taking audibly for granted (like Judy Holliday in *Born Yesterday*, Jadeen thought) the things that everybody knew or felt in common but that nobody, by a law the students obeyed as rigorously as the teachers, ever professed to know or feel in common. Jadeen in her turn was dishonest because the thing, the only thing, she pretended not to know or feel was that this was the universal law.

So she got up abruptly, bounced up, in order to produce that momentary silence, like a giant hiccup, that occurred in the hot whining commotion whenever a teacher, even a pretty substitute teacher who sat in one of those desks not five full

43

years ago, moved. She stepped over Stuart Bordle's legs and sat on the front of the desk, not hiking her skirt up and not pulling it down either, and saying in full voice before the noise had climbed back to its peak:

"Well, do you hate *Hamlet*?"

There was a shocked silence, followed after a few seconds by several wide-eyed oh-no's from the girls, and directly after that by a loud, raggedly chorus of yes's!—some of them testing the edge of impudence, but most of them grateful, even awed.

"O.K.," Jadeen said. "We've got thirty-five minutes left. I'd like to spend it talking about why you hate *Hamlet*. Stuart, why do you?"

There was a silence as before, but a less complete one, broken almost as soon as it began by low hurried conferring. Stuart squirmed and Jadeen let him, knocking her heels negligently against the side of the desk, knowing (as well as Bridget Honeywell, perhaps) the value of an awkward pause.

"Well I mean," Stuart said at last. "All this poetry. Why doesn't the cat say what he means?"

The class broke into skittish laughter and Jadeen said, "All right. For instance." Stuart hid his grin in towards his T-shirt and pulled the open textbook to him, where several specks of Ida Bergen's spittle had not yet dried. He read at deliberate, challenging random, tracing a forefinger under the line and chanting in a flat, slow, sonorous voice:

"And thus the native hue of resolution is sicklied o'er with the pale cast of thought, and enterprises of great pith and moment with this regard their currents turn awry and lose the name of action.' There now. That."

Jadeen nodded with her best Dumb Blonde solemn face. "Well exactly," she said. "Why doesn't he say what he means?

44

—that if a cat is going to dig the scene, he's got to can the gab and get on with it."

"Gab" was wrong, that was old-fashioned, but it didn't matter, they got it. The laughter came this time with a lift of excitement in it, like waking up. Mary Ellen Church said sharply, "No!" and then, forced into emphasis by the attention she had attracted, "But you *could* say it in plain English. Well, *plain* English. You could say . . ."

She frowned impatiently at the text. Jadeen got off the desk and hung her fingers in her pockets, beginning to pace as hands went cautiously up here and there in the room. It would go well now, quickly, and she'd have scored at least one half-hour to the credit of Shakespeare and (don't forget that, either: what was it she said?—"the brief notoriety of a heroine") at the expense of Mrs. Kitchener, Ida Bergen and School at large, to the glorification of herself.

Four o'clock, Hilary

The office of the *Morning Watch*—smaller and politically more liberal of the city's two conservative newspapers, fierce rival of its competitor *Chronicle* even though both were owned and playfully controlled by the same glass-skinned consumptive sugar-cane tycoon—this office stretched for a city block and a half of unadorned grey wall, unrelieved machine clatter and telephone shriek, unremitting pressure of some deadline or other. The windows were beyond a tall man's reach and opened inward on chains, making only the top foot or so of cigar smoke whip and roll. There was no cooling system because Mr. Sasson, the sugar man, who had not been inside the building since 1934, found refrigeration aggravating to the condition of his lungs. There was no water cooler because he was rarely thirsty. There was no acoustical material of any kind, and no partition from the swinging glass doors on the stairwell side all the way back to the small door at the other end, which led to the linotypes and a couple of cubicles where the building seemed reluctantly to concede that a man might relieve himself without the company of his co-workers.

But no one has ever designed a newspaper office in private rooms. The act of making public is no doubt properly performed in public; at least it is true that, except for one disconsolately unmarried file clerk in the morgue and one old columnist who only showed up to proofread himself, each of the inmates of the ugly room was committed to the *Morning Watch* with a proud, jealous, loyal and intensely personal

46

devotion. This is not to be explained. (It was not to be explained, for one, to Dr. Angus Rugg, who said, "Hilary, Hilary, Hilary! . . ." gave up and let him come home from college but never gave in, never allowed him any logic to it at all.)

He sat on the left side as you entered, nearly half-way up towards the city desk, meaning that in eight months he had survived the Obit Pit, Fiftieth Wedding Anniversaries, Episcopal Bingo and the Girl Scout Cookie Drive. Now with three others he covered building, business and the University. He had the south desk in a pinwheel arrangement of four and over his typewriter and Bill Jorgenson's crewcut he could see when, as now, Millar Rourk cast himself sidewards out of his chair at the city desk—the chair continued to swivel around off-centre like a warped record—and bore down through the aisles, cleaving the smoke with his nose.

In spite of himself, in spite of the fact that he was on early shift, his copy was in, and the only duty he had left was to stick around until the first edition went to bed, Hilary automatically clutched at the sheet in his typewriter and ripped it out. He compensated for this failure of style with a grimace towards the crumpled paper now in the basket, indicative of its being badly written, whipped a fresh page in and pursed his mouth at it, contemplative. Rourk came on waving a galley proof like a furled banner. He sat on Hilary's desk and cracked the proof across so that the end of it hung in Hilary's lap.

"Hilary, sweetheart," he said, "I haven't had a chance to say hello to you today."

The complicated arrangement was this: Rourk treated Hilary with exaggerated affection meant to indicate contempt, in order to conceal an overwhelming identification with Hilary as his twenty-year-old self. Hilary treated Rourk with an

47

ironic servility meant to signify disrespect, in order to conceal an admiration that verged on idolatry. Once when Rourk had shown Hilary how to sharpen a news lead by the deletion of a single article, Hilary had said in a slightly nasal boy's voice, "Gee whiz, Mr. Rourk, that's great. I hope I grow up to be just like you." This was too close; both of them had been paralysed with how close it was, and after that Hilary stuck to "Yessiree, sir" and "Anything you say, boss."

He said now, "Hello MisterrOURK, sir," and Rourk smiled a sweet, lightly sarcastic smile. Had Angus Rugg tried to perform such a smile (Hilary knew he made this comparison) he would either have wounded you or bashed you over the head with the fact that he didn't mean it. You would have wanted to avert your eyes from it as from somebody's open fly; whereas with Rourk—the smile flickered out again —you were always wanting to say, wait, hold it, I'd like to study that. You never knew what Rourk was thinking but Hilary had never heard anybody complain that you never knew what Rourk was thinking. On the contrary, that was his quality, that was his style, and what you thought about it generally was that it would have been a welcome quality in a father.

Physically Hilary and Rourk had nothing in common except the central thing, aggressive homeliness. Rourk had a perfectly spherical head with the sheen of new-laid linoleum, and his nose *hung* from it more than anything, like a roof eaves or a brass knocker. Hilary was narrow-skulled and fish-eyed with myopia (that was one thing about Rourk, for instance: he would realize that by the time you were twenty it was no longer hilarious that the great eye doctor had a near-sighted son). And he had his mother's skin, sinewy and pied with uncountable overlapping freckles like a pointillist sketch. It

48

was not much consolation to Hilary to have escaped the acne business because, as he pointed out, he didn't *need* it.

But they had something else in common of which Hilary was only indistinctly aware, and which he was prevented from examining more closely by simple incredulity, as he was vaguely aware of but prevented from examining the fact that Jadeen, like him, mistrusted her own personal success and thought it somehow illgotten: Jadeen! But with Rourk it was something else shared: a manner of dealing with being ugly, of turning it to account, of systematically expunging from your manner any apology or hesitation so that, instead of being by contrast with other men bad-looking, you were by contrast with other bad-looking men very self-possessed. Rourk strode and lunged; Hilary leaned on things; the principle was the same. There were known combinations of audacity and self-deprecation, wit and sentiment, irony and conviction, that automatically, magically made a man lovable and worthy of respect; which came naturally to men with flat ears and shiny teeth but which could be studied and learned as well, as love-making could be studied and learned, which everybody probably agreed but nobody said. But the major and most constant effort always had to be to deny the effort; at all costs not to get caught with the barbells or checking your stance in a mirror. If you were absolutely successful you turned out like Rourk, not so that people no longer thought you ugly but so that nobody, women either, would have wished you otherwise.

"Hello MisterrOURK, sir," Hilary said.

Rourk tapped his blue pencil against the headline on his proof and gave Hilary time to read it over: STRIKES AGAINST THE STEVEDORE. "This is a *sweet* editorial, dear," Rourk said.

"I'm awfully glad you like it. I thought maybe we were

D   49 getting just a mite unbalanced, if you follow me, with all that nasty business about the unions. I thought it might be nice just to sort of even things out."

"It's lovely," Rourk said. His big hands sucked the long sheet up like a string of spaghetti, crumpling it between. Then he lobbed the ball of it sidewards between Hilary's knees neatly into the basket.

"You know, Hilary, this one got past the copy slot, the head writer . . ."

"Nice head," Hilary approved.

". . . the linotype and the slot man again. One of these days one of them is going to get past me and go right out on the streets. And then all these nice people in this room are going to find themselves out on the streets too, looking for work as stevedores I shouldn't doubt."

"Well, yes, sir," Hilary said. "That's why I thought maybe it would be a good idea to make sure the stevedores are getting a buck and a quarter an hour these days."

Bill Jorgenson looked up and grinned, but half irritated because he was trying to get a story done and the two of them were at it again. Rourk saw the irritation and got off Hilary's desk.

"Actually, you know, honey, I'll ask you when I want you to write the editorials for me."

"That's O.K., I don't mind," Hilary said.

Rourk gave him a smile of scathing friendliness and wheeled away. Hilary took the crumpled galley proof from his wastebasket, smoothed it out and slipped it into a drawer with a pile of similarly crumpled and smoothed-out pages—but the rest on ordinary copy paper; this was the first one that had got through to proof. Bill Jorgenson, visibly torn between his deadline and Hilary, set his forearm finally across his keyboard and frowned his perpetual-freshman frown. Jorgenson wore horn-rimmed glasses like Hilary but, unlike Hilary's, they didn't improve him.

"I don't understand what you mean to gain by that, Rugg," Bill Jorgenson said to him. "I mean, old man Sasson's the most reactionary buzzard alive."

"No, is he really? Fancy," Hilary said.

"Well, I mean, why don't you go to work for some other paper though if you don't like the *Watch*'s politics?"

"Name one."

"Well, or up north. I mean, what are you, an agitator?"

Unlike most of his contemporaries, Hilary did not mind arguing with fools, and that, he considered, made him singularly fit to live in the south. But he did mind sharing a decent newspaper with them. I mean, what are you, an agitator?

"Actually," Hilary said, "I'm Sasson's private staff spy, you see. I'm here to keep Rourk up to the mark. If I get through a lead article on Khrushchev's winning the *Watch* citizenship award I get Rourk's job and a lifetime supply of Sasson Sugar Syrup. If I . . ."

"Jesus, Rugg, I've got to get this written."

"Write."

Hilary straightened the sheet in his typewriter and flicked it sharply with his knuckle a couple of times. At this hour of the afternoon the newsroom was filled with fog-thick smoke that seemed to hang in layers of increasing opacity towards the ceiling, but which, like fog, receded as you approached and so was never where you were, only all around you. By some philosophical theory or other this must mean that the smoke did not in fact exist, like sounds where there are no ears, or at least if there was no such philosophy there ought to be. It was impossible to imagine a newsroom without layers of smoke, and it might be that newsmen created it on purpose in order to benefit by the contrast, they dealing in solid, graspable facts that did not recede like fog as you approached. Hilary tapped the sheet again and after a moment's thought he headed it, "Dept. of the Interior—Rugg".

"Debate continued fierce today on the Rugg Age Issue, and prospects for an early settlement seemed dim. Spokesmen predicted that the problem, coming under the Chimerical Dilemmas clause, would not fall in the jurisdiction of the Sane-Sensible-Sagacious Board.

"Committeemember Hilary 'Hi' Rugg recapitulated major points for the press. These are: age of Spatch, college degree of Spatch, independent apartment of Spatch, behaviour (juvenile) of parental Ruggs, and pregnancy of female parental Rugg."

He'd said easily, "I'm nineteen. You're twenty, aren't you?" and when she answered with a little gasp and a blanched face, "Oh! No, twenty-one!" he'd laughed—he'd planned to laugh, but he felt it too, she was so solemn and concerned—and had taken the car up to eighty-five on the throughway till he had her scared, ducked off to the edge of the river and stopped and kissed her hard, saying nothing before or after and she didn't either but she got the message, that he was the older and the leader and they'd have no more discussion on *that*.

It had worked absolutely. That's the thing about Jadeen, she was teachable. It had worked so well that now it didn't even amuse her when anybody noticed it, she'd got past even that and only shrugged. It was Hilary who'd begun avoiding the names of people at Centre who were after her class or before his. It was he who had begun to point out—she shrugged at this as well, not even aware that he was belittling her—that her teacher's diploma was a "certificate", not a "degree". It was he who regretted, brooded, that they had never slept anywhere else than her apartment, before; as if Jadeen's taking a place of her own had been not only an invitation but also an admonishment. Yet this was wholly unlike Jadeen and, besides, these things hadn't caused but had come in the wake of a discomfort that had been growing in him since, since . . .

Since the Ruggs took her in like she was a puppy, just nuts about her, well, what a love! And Hilary, standing astonished on the sidelines, wishing to say: This is Miss Spatch of Noon Street, My Betrothéd: watched the three of them making what they called friends in hysterical high spirits, like people in a movie run at double speed. Maeve setting her straight to work in the kitchen and Angus (Do call me Angus!) padding about after them in his slippers telling interminable jokes and shooting congratulatory epithets sideways to Hilary.

He had wished them to be dignified, learned, impressive, as when they entertained the Governor or a foreign doctor; he felt betrayed that they played this comedy, and not less so that Jadeen took it so happily, saying "Maeve" and "Angus" from the first and learning to announce, "'Scuse me, I have to pee," in exactly that tone of boastful objectivity with which his father had been exasperating him since he was twelve. So that his mother's pregnancy itself had seemed a part of some jolly conspiracy to cut Jadeen off from him and graft her on to them. Instead of the grave wonder that Hilary felt at the idea of a forty-year-old woman with a twenty-year-old son having another baby, Maeve and Angus—and perforce Jadeen— simply began to act as if Maeve were *not* a forty-year-old woman. His parents ogled each other and rubbed knees on the sly, Angus puffed up and gave Hilary knowing winks when he managed to embarrass Jadeen, Maeve refused to buy more than one maternity dress ("Wherever would I *wear* them?") and went about the house in Angus's cast-off sport shirts, she and Jadeen giggled like schoolgirls over Hilary's baby pictures. He had always disliked the idea of his infancy, where he existed only in memories other than his own, and when he had been therefore not really himself but only an object in the possession and power of a whole unchosen crew of relatives. Furthermore, he had always particularly admired his mother because she was *not* one of those that pulled out the album every time he brought home a girl. But now! She was quite capable of describing his intra-uterine personality to Jadeen at the dinner table, and Jadeen just as willing to be charmed by it as if she were not in a couple of hours going to climb in bed with the foetal acrobat. All right, but if his mother was not a forty-year-old woman, what did that make Hilary?

He straightened the page again and flipped the carriage bar.

"Regarding the final point, Rugg remarked, 'When a forty-year-old man becomes a grandfather, he feels fifty. When a twenty-year-old man becomes a brother, he feels ten.' Applause and cries of 'hear, hear' followed the lanky former second vice president of the Centre High Swim Seven to his seat.

"Debate was opened by H. G. 'Hug' Rugg, one-time mumblety-peg magnate, who pointed out the relevance of Dr. Sigmund ('Si') Freud. Said Rugg, 'Sibling rivalry and all that.' Larry 'Bug' Rugg quickly countered with a motion to strike this argument from the records. 'Crap,' commented the smiling former two-penny lemonade salesman. Sharp debate ensued between Doug 'Dug' Rugg, con, and, the pro faction consisting of Shrug Rugg, Shag Rug and Abednigo.

"Rugg charged that Rugg was 'still bugged' by Miss Spatch's excess two years two months, and that he was 'going to rake up that old . . .'"

"Hilary, honey."

Hilary started and felt his muscles begin to squeeze before he took control of them, set one elbow on the typewriter carriage and, thus obscuring his page, looked languidly up at Rourk.

"I've got a nasty little job for you, I'm afraid." ·

Rourk had a heavy southern voice with a joke always lurking in it. Jorgenson had gone off with his copy, and Rourk plopped himself in that chair, cattycorner from Hilary and lower now so that the danger was less of his looking at what was on the page, even if he'd wanted to, which he never had yet, and what difference would it have made anyway? Still, Hilary found that his forearm stuck and the best he could do (he did this pretty well) was to add the other to it in a long stretch and then fold the arms and set his chin on them, mock-eager.

"Seems like a couple of your picket friends down at the dock have run into trouble with the bystanders, who aren't bystanding any longer. . . ."

Stung with hope, Hilary lifted his head, and Rourk frowned, sorry (as Hilary instantly realized) to have misled him.

"I couldn't send you, baby," he said. "I couldn't trust you any." His thick red neck got shorter, like a turtle's, and he smiled apologetically, without sarcasm this time. But, "The facts," burst from Hilary before he could stop himself, "the whole facts and nothing but the facts so help me Sasson. I'm the only person you've got who can get you quotes from both sides, Rourk. I swear to God . . ."

He broke off as Rourk turned away and picked up a functionless slab of metal from Jorgenson's desk; something too light to be a paperweight and too big to be a fob ornament, with the crest of some very second-rate fraternity glued in the middle of it. Rourk studied the Greek inscription on this for a moment and then, not smiling this time but turning directly to Hilary as if for the first time in eight months he knew the weight of anything he said, Rourk said again, "I couldn't trust you."

He could have protested but it would have been wrong. The most important thing is not to get caught with the bar-bells. He shrugged slightly but without being capable of the facial expression that goes with a shrug, and said only, "O.K." Rourk too was unhappy and, not bothering with their game, he said dully, "Mendick's covering it, and I'll need him to stick around there tonight. But he *was* going to cover your dad's speech for the meds. I'm sorry, but you're the only one I've got to do it."

"Oh, my God, Rourk!" Hilary ripped the page out of his typewriter—knowing, noticing that he could take this oppor-tunity to get rid of it—and smashed it savagely. "In the first place I'm not on tonight. And in the second place I've got a date. And in the third place I've been listening to his speeches every night at the dinner table since I was two years old. I won't even be able to *hear* it!"

It was too vehement. Neither of them knew quite where it had come from, and they sat for a moment looking at each other over Jorgenson's college souvenir in an inattentive anguish that made the room seem suddenly very still, although it was not.

"It'll be good for you," Rourk said at last, almost sullenly. "Look for Andy Dodds from I.P. If he isn't there you can write the story tomorrow. If he is we'll have to have it by midnight for the last edition. It doesn't look good for us to carry a local story from I.P."

Hilary said nothing.

"If Dodds is there we need the copy by midnight. Thousand words, no more. No later."

It wasn't often that Rourk took refuge in a simple order, and as he plunged back down towards the city desk Hilary felt, among all the other things, a kind of astonished pride. A failure was more than most men had shared with Millar Rourk.

Five o'clock, Rugg

Rugg's last appointment was late. His desk was stacked with all de Sevres's monographs and his own, which Miss Stimpson set out when he had a speech to make as regularly as Maeve put the catsup on the table, knowing he'd given up using it long ago, but out of a habit by now almost dignified into tradition.

He lay the pamphlets in three bumpy lines over the litter on his desk: de Sevres's, his translations of de Sevres, his own later refinements on graft and suture methods. The inspiration, the idea, had been de Sevres's. He gave him credit, but he'd always regretted and, well, all right, resented, that the primary material went exclusively to de Sevres. If he'd been allowed free access to their joint experiments he might have saved five or six years later. De Sevres was old and he might have thought of that; but he wouldn't, not de Sevres. An enormous man, with hands so big that one thumb-nail eclipsed a whole exposed eyeball as he worked on it. He'd said, "I do not wish to be distracted. You convince and deal with them; I shall study the results. I do not wish ever to see a prisoner except under anaesthesia." And he hadn't, either. Rugg was shocked at the time but now he only remembered that he had been shocked, he couldn't call up the force of it. All he retained in force was the regret of not having those first reports, not even knowing where in the Allied military archives they might be buried.

They'd told him to pick his own subject for tonight, so

Rugg did pick it: he closed his eyes and let his forefinger fall on one of the monographs. Penicillin to preserve corpse eyes. Fine. That was an exciting story and not too technical for the new first-years. He could make it a bit ghoulish to begin with and get them interested.

He shuffled the pamphlets up together—including the penicillin one; he didn't need it—and was setting them back in their glass bookcase when he finally realized that something was bothering him. Something big and out of focus, as if it were just on the edge of his range of vision. His mind turned in to it slowly. It was nearly five o'clock, he hadn't thought of it for about four hours. Bejeezus, wasn't that interesting. How many times had he left to open the Med School evening series? Maybe he had better decide on some less arbitrary way of picking his topics. Or tell the whole story tonight, in outline, all the way from that first interview with de Sevres right down to today's last appointment with—who was it? He took up the folder on his desk. Oh, yes, with Andrew Dodds, poor bastard.

He cleared a space in the middle of the desk and spread out the contents of the folder, green and white sheets and salmon-coloured cards delineating, in a lab technician's meticulous script and his own explosive one, the incredible multiplicity of Dodds's optical misfortune. Cataract, leucomata, glaucoma, diabetic lesions of the retinal vessels. Hopeless, hopeless. So little vision on the perimeter of the left eye that he'd be seeing things in two dimensions unless he looked at them head on. Not that much of a range in the other, either, and narrowing all the time, right down to the centre blind spot on the right cornea. Hopeless.

Well, but all the same, theoretically, how much could you do about it? Rugg put his eye-model on the desk in the middle

59

of the papers and puckered his mouth at it for a minute. Then he went into his bathroom and brought out Mama Lily's other eye from where he'd stuck it on the shelf, and lined that up beside the first one. Mama Lily's was smaller, which looked odd, and they were both right eyes, but that only showed in the muscles, and there was nothing wrong with Dodds's muscles. Now. Students always seemed to have the eerie feeling that their replicas were looking at them, at least at first. With Rugg it was just the opposite, and a good deal more unnerving as far as he could tell: a trick of seeing entire any eyeball that focused on him, the whole white globe with its little cap like a saucer in front, and the tail of nerve running backward up into the brain. Maeve's with that unearthly Irish-blue iris leaping up in cross section every time he went to kiss her. And especially Hilary's, *seeing* those light rays meet too far forward and just wanting to push on them, deflect them with his hands; which Hilary showed he sensed by taking his eyes away, not timidly or guiltily away but with a great rude angry jerk. Angry that his father couldn't do it, that he was an eye doctor at all, that he was his father, something, whatever.

Now.

The cataract to begin with, the left one was almost ripe, leave the sack, slit it and remove the lens, right. He patched up the split layer of Mama Lily's eye with some Scotch tape and drew the incision on it with a lead pencil. Now. He stood tapping his pencil on the ciliary tissue working out ahead like a chess move whether the keratoplasty or the iridectomy ought to come next. The sound of his pencil bothered him again, and he stopped it when he realized why: Trippin's pencil on the X-ray frame, sounding the same but meaning something else, something prim and admonitory like eight hours sleep

60

and plenty of fresh air. God, that Trippin was an ass. He probably spanked his children for getting cavities in their teeth.

That was a weird thing, his sitting here now with Dodds coming (or maybe not coming; it was two minutes to five; maybe he knew what the news was and had decided not to come) just as Trippin had sat at noon waiting for him. This chilled him because all he felt towards Dodds was a clinical respect of his case and the most generalized sort of pity. But Trippin had known him since they went to Centre High together, and he'd only seen Dodds once, had nothing in common with him except that his son had picked the same silly profession. If he hadn't been generally moved by the plight of the potential blind he would have gone into some other branch of medicine, and if he'd been individually and specifically moved by it he'd be emotionally paralysed by now. Ataxia of the empathetic nerve, like Trippin, who undoubtedly knew a lot about the heart but hadn't learned that if there was one thing a man had a right to do, it was to choose how he wanted to take bad news. The messenger boy could just adjust himself to it or get out. But not Trippin, sitting there tight-faced as if he were rehearsing for some war-movie (they always made the doctors look *brave*: Rugg couldn't figure out what the doctors had to be so brave about) and grimly explaining the function of the heart in words of one syllable as if Rugg was a mason or a storekeeper, not telling him any more than he learned in Zoology 1B when he was nineteen. Rugg had said, "That looks shot all right. That doesn't look as if it could pump water out of Old Faithful," and Trippin stopped the pencil for a minute, his mouth making a stiff little O as if Rugg had been insulting Trippin's heart instead of his own. Trippin could give lessons to an undertaker. That was one thing he

had to offer Dodds as consolation, at least, that he wasn't
going to put on one of those phony undertaker faces, nor the
war-movie act either. But my God, what *had* Trippin been
feeling? Something more than usual, something to represent
thirty-plus years of proximity and common purpose? Or just
the nervousness, as usual, like this, like this he felt about that
poor bastard Dodds.

Miss Stimpson knocked crisply on the door and came three-
quarters of the way in, leaving one leg behind the way that
had seemed so cute ten-fifteen years ago.

"Mr. Dodds, doctor. Shall I tell him you've gone home?"

Gone home? Gone home? "Why should you tell him I've
gone home?"

"Well, he's half an hour late. I thought . . ."

"No, no, Janet, thanks. I'll see him."

Miss Stimpson went out. Gone home! These northern
minds worked in the oddest way. Every time Miss Stimpson
found one of his patients insufficiently respectful, Rugg
thanked his stars again that nothing ever came of that. There'd
been the inevitable time at first, two people sharing the same
set of rooms forty hours a week, when just their crossing back
and forth so often generated sparks between them. She was
younger than Maeve, too, then; and now she was so much
older she was old enough to be, if not Maeve's mother, at least
the baby's grandmother. Maeve had that from the Irish, the
not ageing; and the pale iris, and that was all, except for a
general indifference to things like *tidiness* and *tact* that Rugg
considered, from having watched his colleague's wives pin
antimacassars and change subjects, easily the most rare and
amenable quality in a woman. And that made him glad
nothing had ever come of it with Miss Stimpson.

He turned the two plastic eyes around on his desk so that

62

they faced the door, but that put Mama Lily's on the right, and he'd already drawn the incision on it for the left one, so he traded them around. Dodds came in wiping his neck and shivering a little from the air conditioning; he looked from one plastic eye to the other and blinked when Rugg stuck his hand out between them where the nose would have been, but came forward finally and shook it.

He was as tall as Grappap, with a large long head, the features set low in it and the skin, the mealy skin of a diabetic, draped about them in deep loops. A cocker spaniel face, down to the way the flesh slouched over the outer eye and the jowls hung with a look of insufferable sorrow. Like a spaniel's, his face would have looked that way even if he'd had an easy life, but he hadn't. Carried his insulin around with him in a cigarette case, Hilary said, and begrudged the time off to give himself an injection. He could have had pretty near any newspaper job he wanted, but he picked the I.P. night beat because he couldn't sleep at night. But whatever hour things happened, according to Hilary, that was the hour that Dodds just happened to be on; he materialized where news was as if he was brought into being by it, and he was always last to leave and first with the copy in. Where there was an accident he knew the names of the survivors before the dead were pronounced dead.

Having him here now at last Rugg felt overtired and jumpy. I could just do without this part of it, he thought. I know what de Sevres meant and I guess by now I share it. I don't mind cutting into an eye, I even still like it, but I don't like watching it take the news.

"Sorry I'm late," Dodds said, "but there's been a kind of a picket riot down at the docks, and I had to wait to be relieved. I couldn't get a cab . . ."

63

"That so? Never mind. Sit down, sit down . . ." Rugg waved him to a chair and Dodds sat, looking up from under those hanging eyebrows, tense with waiting. A big man looks worse nervous than a small one, more of himself not to know what to do with.

"Matter of fact," Rugg said, "I've been using the time to work out my plan of attack. You're a phenomenon, I can tell you. The things you haven't got would make a slim book. You could go into a circus."

Dodds laughed in short shallow breaths, letting some of the tension out and ending up with a sheepish-proud smile. He'd learned that early on. You tell people that what they've got is something special and they mind it a lot less.

"I've set the models up to explain it to you, they're not near as pretty as your eyes but they're in better shape. Some of the things are happening on both sides and some on only one, so I'll take them one at a time in the order I'd tackle them. Stop me if you miss something, or if I get too technical."

Dodds hitched himself forward in his chair and rubbed his lips together, ready to concentrate. Rugg remembered hitching forward on Trippin's chair—Trippin's was a high-backed ugly carved chair, though, and this one was plain and graceful —and he felt struck, stopped, frozen by seeing Dodds do it. There were the framed diplomas on the wall, the cooling vents, the electric wall clock, the glass bookcase and the great block of mahogany desk, all the same as Trippin's except that Trippin's chairs were carved and high-back. Trippin's eyebrow had gone up, synchronized with his pencil going down on the valve in a diagram. Why had Trippin looked *superior* while he was explaining it? What was the purpose of that?

"Now to begin with you've got a couple of dandy cataracts going. Only the left one is ripe yet, so we'd start by getting rid

64

of that. You can think of the lens as one of those closed plastic ice cubes—you know the kind?—the stuff inside freezes and melts without diluting your drink? Right, well, the lens of the eye is shaped like a flying saucer but in consistency it's more like one of those ice cubes. There's a tough membrane around it with liquid inside, and if the liquid starts to harden it crystallizes like ice. I know more than one fellow's tried to look at the world through a bunch of ice cubes, and I can tell you it doesn't work."

Dodds laughed again, not probably that he thought that so funny but that he was loosening up, he was more cheerful than when he arrived, and that was the second difference from Trippin's, after the high-back chairs.

"So once it's hard enough to come out in one piece we just slit down through the cornea and the membrane and pick it out with a pair of fancy tweezers."

His pencil made a slightly zipping sound tracing over the incision he'd already drawn on Mama Lily's eye, and Dodds winced.

"Now come on, don't get squeamish yet, that's not the beginning. There's nothing to that, I could do a couple of those before breakfast every morning."

Dodds went sheepish-looking again, his smile deepening still further the line of those hanging jowls.

"That'd give you the third dimension back—because now, you know, you're seeing just about boo out of that eye. But then there's something else creeping up on you on both sides. You've got a slow glaucoma—that's why sunlight bothers you —which means that your whole eye is hardening little by little, the pupil doesn't react quick and it doesn't react far. Ordinarily, your range of vision includes both sides in a hundred-and-eighty-degree angle like an open fan. With a

E   65 glaucoma the fan simply starts to close, narrowing your range down all the time. One thing we could do is just to cut a bigger hole for you to see out of: take a kind of a doughnut shape out of that wicked green iris: so." Smiling, he indicated a swift ring on the iris layer of Mama Lily's model, and this time Dodds swallowed and nodded instead of wincing.

"Now there's a serious difference of opinion about glaucoma. It doesn't happen suddenly, and in about nine cases out of ten you're dead before you get round to going blind. On the whole I'm for leaving it alone. But you've got the works, you're the berries. Because you see you've also got a white spot here in the middle of the right cornea, just where you'd have any vision left when the glaucoma got done with you. If the glaucoma don't get you the leucoma will." Rugg laughed, prompting, at his own joke.

"Jesus Christ," Dodds said very quietly without moving his lips at all, and then immediately he too laughed, an I-give-up snort, accepting, entering into Rugg's mood, which at the same time he badly threatened by saying Jesus Christ, bringing up Rugg's reflection in the phone booth with the red slat slicing across his face. He felt the same fuzz in his mouth and the same sense of not being able to fix his attention.

"It's just a very good thing for you you've got that, though, now," Rugg said shifting the eye models closer together and farther apart again and then sitting sideways on the desk so that he was talking more or less over his shoulder to Dodds and his pencil was going noiselessly up and down on his knee. "Because that's my specialty and I'm very fond of people who've got it. I helped invent this operation twenty years ago, it's a real beauty and I do a splendid job of it—pity you couldn't watch. First you see we'd have to find a nice fresh eye that somebody hasn't got any use for any more, and then

66

cut a piece out of the very outer layer of it with a thingamajig that works on the principle of an apple-corer and cost about as much as my car. Then I'd take the spotted piece out of your cornea with the same whatchamacallit, it's called a trepan if you're interested, and slip the clear one in and sew it in place with eight superfine dressmaker stitches."

"Sounds great," Dodds said. He offered Rugg a cigarette—after a moment's hesitation Rugg refused—and lit one for himself, his hands shaking slightly but his face fine, his legs slung one over the other carelessly. "And then is that the lot?"

"That's all the operating," Rugg answered. "You'd still have lesions of the vessels in your retina both sides, from the diabetes."

"And what do we do about that?"

Rugg shook his head and drew a little spurt of air in on one side of his mouth. "Well, nothing, really."

"Nothing?" Dodds's head came up and the smoke he was about to exhale disappeared somewhere inside, never came out. "Is it serious?"

"Well, now," Rugg said, working the hinged eyelid on Mama Lily's eye up and down, "there are drops and injections and so forth. If we do all the rest of that stuff we could probably keep it under control five, maybe ten years."

"Let me understand you," Dodds said sharply. "Are you saying that in five-maybe-ten years I'll be blind *anyway*?"

"Funny thing is," Rugg answered, "that for a long time they blamed insulin for the lesions before somebody finally pointed out that diabetics had never lived that long before. It's the disease's fault, not the cure's. You're probably very much aware that fifty years ago you'd never have got to the ripe old age of forty-four at all, you . . ."

Dodds was staring at him and it happened to Rugg again,

67

he saw the eyeballs entire and exposed, every layer of the globes flawed or clouded: the cornea flecked and the pupil hardening, narrowing, the lens turning into splintery crystals and the blood-vessels spreading out and running little alien red shoots into the retina. Rugg could see he was going to be one of the ones that took it hard, Dodds was. He would never quite get hold of the miracle of his simply being alive, or of his being given five more years of sight. People have got used to that kind of miracle, they no longer say, "Can you really do it?"—they say, "Do you have to *operate?*" You spend thirty years fighting a certain kind of physical failure and then everybody who's got it blames you for it because it's your specialty, it's yours, as if you invented it. Rugg was glad for having made it a little easier, for having got the light-hearted reaction he was after, but now all of a sudden he felt defeated. He'd have liked to tell Dodds about Trippin, to have said, "You just don't know when you're lucky. We can give you five years for sure. They can't give me anything for sure, not two blessed hours for certain." He had a sudden wild wish that Dodds really was a spaniel. He would have liked to let his own face fall into a pile of loose-skin fur. In fact Dodds's skin seemed to be hardening into its folds, like stalactites forming on a cave wall. He was going to take it hard.

Six o'clock, Maeve

One thing Maeve had never understood was how the bags she brought the groceries home in could be too small to hold the garbage from the same groceries. She sat in the kitchen in the slung canvas chair, her weight on the tail of her spine the way she was supposed to avoid, but too comfortable to move, looking at a pile of coffee grounds and corn husks on the sink. If she didn't clean the sink off before Angus got home and she had to rush the supper on to the table because of his speech, she'd regret it. But she was out of bags and she'd have to go all the way up front into his den to find an old newspaper. This seemed an illogical expenditure of labour because logically the bags ought to hold all the garbage with room to spare, even though they never did, and every Tuesday night she had to go up to the den and hunt up an old newspaper.

It was the national demon at work, she supposed. Never sufficient receptacles for the refuse. Never enough bags for the garbage, tenements for the poor, hospital beds for the sick, marriages for the children, sea for the sewage. They'd had to close up Lake Charlebeau this summer because the fish appeared on the surface one day, millions of them dead and bloated, polluted nobody knew how and they hadn't found out yet. In Ireland life was harder and only, she knew, from a distance a more attractive kind of hard. There people crawled over the little land and died off of it, they and their belongings disappearing into the peat and leaving only little rows of displaced stone like scratches. Here they took a big land and

69

made it bigger, splitting off chunks of it called "raw" materials and frothing them up like egg whites into things and things and things until the very mountains had mountains on them and there would never be any place, anywhere, to put all the junk.

Ah, mountainous me, Maeve thought sitting on her tail bone and cupping her arms lightly around the mound in the middle of her. Being pregnant is like being drunk, however you are it makes you more so. I have got to wrap that garbage. But if Angus had repaired the porch screen I could have left this chair out there and then it wouldn't be in the kitchen where I can fall into it and not get out of it, therefore if I have to clear space to set up the plates after he gets here and he's late to his lecture it will be his fault.

Angus.

She was waiting for Angus, which was her profession. For twenty-two years she had been waiting for Angus once a day six days a week, twice when he had something on in the evening, which was usually, and if he came home for lunch that made it three times, an absorbing and exhausting occupation. In one way of looking at it, she was a profoundly disappointed woman and this was a disappointing marriage, because Angus had been disappointing her with his home-coming once, twice or three times a day for twenty-two years. But it wasn't his fault. It was the quality of her waiting, the only thing she had to put her intensity into so that the days he didn't come home to lunch, by six o'clock so much of it had accumulated that he'd have had to come in on a pogo stick or a zebra for it not to be a letdown. She had no talent and no fondness for housework, and this big old place never left her time for much of anything else, so that there had to be a focal point for all of it, some goal to every silly little task, which couldn't very well be anything else than Angus's homecoming even if she had not anyway instinctively and perpetually acted, behaved, with reference to Angus. Every tubful of laundry, every room's worth of dusting, she thought, this will be done when Angus gets home, even though she knew that she would never have the house *clean* any of the times Angus came home because she wasn't that kind of woman; and even though she knew that if she had Angus would not notice it. She'd tried cleaning-women but that wasn't in her either. If anything she waited worse. She went around the house from room to room to avoid the woman, her finger in a book she wasn't reading anyway, desperate not to pass her in the halls and dropping her eyes with a forced smile when she did so, feeling like a little girl playing mistress of the house and once, when she came in through the screen porch and found the girl scrubbing stains out of the crotch of her, Maeve's, nylon panties, simply bursting into tears of shame and telling Angus that night, "I can't have anyone working for me, that's all, I can't. Someday I'll try to apologize by telling her about digging peat, and how bad it was when the donkey died, and make a fool of myself for you. I can't, that's all."

Every time Hilary said he was going to get an apartment in town they talked about moving to someplace smaller, one of the new split-levels across the bay, or build on Angus's bayou lot. But they couldn't do that either, it seemed; they needed high ceilings and all-but-unsweepable crannies and comfortable old rooms with dust-catching cornices to put all their dust-catching gewgaws in, Angus's bargains. Unnecessary space was necessary to them. When Maeve thought about it, she really didn't particularly admire an efficient kitchen, or want one anyway. So they stayed where they were and then, after all—Hilary saw it too—there was no sense in Hilary's

71

going into town and paying half his salary for more *rooms*, and leaving them with one more here. They could let him have two or three more rooms, if that's what he wanted, but it wasn't. He could have Jadeen into any room he picked and lock the door as long as he liked, too, if that's what he wanted, but it wasn't that either. They would never know what Hilary wanted, and one of the great differences between Maeve and Angus was that Maeve had accepted this and no longer worried about it or tried to figure out what it was. She had never learned not to kiss him too much, not to hold him struggling when he was seven and eight, so she'd made this her hobby, as waiting for Angus was her profession, not wanting to know what Hilary wanted, even of her. She was rewarded. He felt it. He didn't have to define it or justify it with her and so they got on better than he and Angus. Once passing the open living-room door where Hilary was sitting with Jadeen, she'd heard the words ". . . my mother as a person . . ." and she'd walked on smiling, *very* rewarded by that, and amused. Young people were always so taken with the idea of seeing their parents *as people* separate from themselves that it never occurred to them the *people* might have the same difficulty seeing their children that way.

She heard the gravel-scattering wheeze of the Packard in the drive, a hole in its windpipe somewhere, and the noise gave her impetus at last. She shoved herself up out of the chair and took off her apron because it looked so odd riding her great belly like that. Suddenly there were a dozen things besides the garbage that had to be done instantly. She twisted the damp hairs on her neck and poked them up into her bun. Goodness it was hot. She'd never thought to spend another summer pregnant, and such a summer! The hairs fell again. Some women could keep all their hair in a bun. Some women

72

could go all day and at evening have the same clear hairline they'd brushed everything back from in the morning. Jadeen, even when she came in out of the wind, looked as if her waves had been painted that way to tumble on her wind-pink cheeks. Sweet Jadeen.

The water was already boiling with the spices in the biggest soup-pot. She went to the sink and selected the most accessible of the eight live eye-blue crabs that were scrabbling over each other and trying to climb the enamel sinksides; grasped it expertly between thumb and forefinger just behind the furiously snapping claws, carried it the ten steps across to the stove and dropped it in the boiling water.

Maeve supposed there must be something wrong with her to be so fond of her only son's fiancée, especially seeing that Angus was half in love with her as well. Angus made a certain gesture, flexing his palm, when Jadeen came in, that Maeve recognized as a symbolic grab for flesh. But it was that kind of skin, Jadeen's. Maeve would have liked to rub it too. That was being pregnant, probably, and being pregnant was probably why she was giving Hilary up so easily.

The crab sank instantly, bright red before it hit bottom, reminding her, as always, of the litmus paper in the abortive basic science course that Angus had tried to give her just after they were married. She went back for the second, the third; it probably *was* inefficient to make eight ten-step trips and back to get eight crabs from the sink to the stove, but she was supposed to walk, and a crab wasn't such bad company if you held him right. The seventh, the eighth, the screen porch door.

Wham!

"Hello there! Maeve, m'love?"

There he was, was she ready? She grimaced ruefully at the

73

unwrapped garbage, the dark liquid from the grounds seeping through the floss and gathering in ugly pools in the husks. Ugh. Someday when Angus got home she would be ready for him, as well as impatient. Tomorrow.

"Hello, sweetheart," she called.

He came swinging in, carrying a box that looked cubical in the brief glance she had of it, his coat limp over his arm and his shirt sticking to him wherever his undershirt didn't cover, saying "Bejeezus," with reference to the weather, putting his arms around her and leaning exaggeratedly in to her over her belly, saying, "Some parts of the world they call September *autumn*," and kissing her and then saying, "I find you practically inaccessible these days"; all before she had had time simply to register his presence, which she would like to have done slowly, leisurely, at arm's length first.

Angus asked her, still leaning in and the corner of his box poking into her shoulder blade, "Did you go to the doctor?"

"Uh-hmm."

"Well, what about my boy?"

She faced him gravely and said, "Angus, the doctor says that the foetus is directly upside down."

He looked startled and worried for a second, that second that was her day's goal and triumph because she had been saving this joke up and practicing it over for him ever since she got home. His face relaxed gradually, and he laughed and gave her a sly look, and then it was over, the best that she could expect from this homecoming. It was almost—it was always almost—enough.

"Coming out head first, is he, the little bastard?" Angus said. "And otherwise? Varicosities? Anaemia? . . . Heart? That old worn out body taking it all right?"

"I'll thank *you*!" Maeve said. "If you think my body's so

74

worn out what makes you put babies in it? We stringy types can outlast half a dozen of you Sunday afternoon athletes."

He folded his face down into her neck and started kissing her there along the collarbone and (she was so familiar with the way he did things, the order he did them in and the kind of transition he made from one to another) she was suddenly, irrationally, alarmed.

"What's the matter, Angus?"

"Nothing, I'm tired," he said. He looked up again and smiled at her and, really, he did look tired, the vertical lines on his forehead deep, and hollows at the inside corners of his eyes, making his nose seem even sharper.

"I had to tell somebody he was going blind this afternoon. It takes more energy to say that than to say anything else I know."

"Poor Angus."

"And I haven't really decided what I'm going to talk about tonight. I thought the penicillin part of it, but . . ."

He was starting to slip away from her already now, backwards and forwards from this moment that was hers, back into what he had done at the Centre all day and forward to what he would do at the medical school this evening and in the operating room tomorrow morning. Her having him to herself was done already, and she felt the disappointment coming over her, familiar as dishwater. But a little less oppressive now maybe because she had the other, the baby, to wait for as well.

"What are you poking me in the back with, Angus?"

"Wellah, yes, now." He stepped back from her, creating sudden eddies of Crabboil in the smell of his sweat, and tossed his jacket into the canvas chair. He held the box out on his palm and took off the lid: the sides fell all at once on

75

hinges around his hand, Angus loved that kind of thing. It was one of those eyes, a piece gone out of it and all marked up with pencil, in bad shape really.

"Oh, Angus. Angus Rugg. Have you been to Mama Lily's? Whatever did you pay for that?"

That was the beginning of an argument if she wasn't careful, and there wasn't time to get all the way through one before Hilary and Jadeen came, and afterwards he'd have to go right off, so she'd better be careful. Economy affected Angus like the English had affected her father.

"Now, Maeve, let's not start that. We've got enough money that if I want to *give away* . . ."

"Five dollars, Angus?" She hadn't meant to say it, it came automatically, out of the memory of having put two five-dollar bills in his wallet this morning. She'd rather it cost twenty dollars than have this argument they were heading into, but really, it wasn't her fault if pregnant women were cranky, and a little of the responsibility lay on him to allow for it.

"Never *mind* what it cost, Maeve."

"Oh, all right, but for heaven's sake, why *that*?"

He was still holding it out on his palm, but he lowered it now and looked at it for a minute before answering. "Hilary had one," he said. "I thought his little brother ought to have one too."

She was terribly touched. She felt the tears springing up with her surprise, that Angus should remember that, that Angus should do something so sentimental as that. But those easy tears, even though they were a part of being pregnant too, did irritate him so, and his eyes were already sliding off, furtive, embarrassed by his answer.

So she clacked her tongue loudly and said, "Angus, I'm awfully sorry to disappoint you, but this is a little girl-foetus and her name is Dareena. She'll love the eyeball, dear. Put it in her room."

She turned away and stirred the crabs with a long wooden spoon; it wouldn't occur to Angus that there's no point in stirring crabs. Then when everything was all right with her eyes she turned back and tossed him his jacket again.

"Hang that up, now. I've ironed the olive for tonight. And a *clean* white shirt, Angus. Oh, and Angus, there's a dear, would you run up to your den and get me a newspaper for the garbage first?"

Seven o'clock, Rugg

After he gave her the paper he took the eye model up to the little room, cattycorner across the hall from theirs, that Maeve had chosen for the baby. It was full of newness and disorder. If he was born tomorrow he would have a print of Picasso's *Child with Pigeon* in a freshly hand-honeyglazed frame, but no bed. Hilary's old crib—she could have had all new things if she'd wanted, but she actively didn't so he hadn't pressed it—lay dismantled on newspapers all over the floor, one slat making a paint spot where it leaned against the new wallpaper, the footboard flat in the middle with the brush strokes simply stopping half-way down. The brush was glued to a corner of the newspaper and the can was open, scum hardening on the top. Clearly the telephone had rung.

Rugg put the lid on the can and the brush in the turpentine jar and folded up a piece of curtain that was hanging off the sewing-machine into the paint. He took the eye out of its box and set it on the window sill, then moved it to the bureau, then back to the window sill again. He set the box down just anywhere, but couldn't quite leave and stood smelling the paint, looking at the bright jumble of preparation and Mama Lily's eye that seemed so out of place in it; more out of place here than it would in any of the other, darker and more settled rooms.

He felt an acute sheepishness about that, Maeve's whole face contracting with pleasure so sharp that it might have been pain instead, and her turning away to poke at the crabs so he

78

wouldn't see it. He always felt guilty when he had done anything *affective* with Maeve, and this was worse than usual
because there was no good reason not to tell her why he had
really bought it. Maeve wasn't ungenerous, it was waste she
hated, and if she heard the story she would be capable of
understanding not only his giving ten dollars for the model
but, what most women would not, his anguish about doing it.

But it was such a long story; he really had to change. And it
would only have mollified her, not moved her, delighted her,
as this had done. She'd notice it now if he didn't leave it here,
and be genuinely disappointed. Still.

He made an impatient gesture and, leaving the box where-
ever it was, picked the battered eye up by its pedestal and
took it with him into their bedroom, where he stuck it on the
lower shelf of the nightstand. He decided that he could do
without another shave and that if he couldn't he'd have to
anyway. He took a quick icy shower and got into the dark
green suit that he saved for speeches in the summer because it
seemed to hold its shape better against his flexings and flail-
ings. Tying his tie he looked out of the window and saw
Hilary's car pull up, a sharp little red and black MG that Rugg
had given him to go to college in and that he'd fully intended
to make Hilary pay for when he quit to go to work, though
he'd never got round to telling him so.

Hilary slammed out and took his time coming around to
open Jadeen's door, so that she'd done it for herself by the
time he got there. They were fighting evidently. He leaned an
elbow on the roof and supported his head on it in a patient,
exasperated way. Jadeen, tiny beside him in a tube of bright
white linen and a red belt, worked her hands one grasp at a
time along the top of a handbag the size of a whole black kid,
frowning up at him, flushed. They started up the walk, talking

79

excitedly, and Rugg put on his jacket, his shoes last, and went downstairs.

Maeve was clattering things on to the table in the dining-room, and he could hear them still in the entry hall.

"It doesn't matter, Hilary, it's only an hour. Why don't we go on afterwards? I've got to go to my mother's anyway."

"I don't see why—hold still, I don't see anything."

"It's on the bottom, more towards the centre."

"I don't see why you've got to go to your mother's."

"Because, Hilary . . ."

"There it is, ash or something."

"Because I want to do everything exactly as she said, and then I'll have been just as fair about it as possible, don't you see . . . Hilary, that's a *filthy* handkerchief!"

Jadeen had her back against the mirror, and Hilary was propped in front of her on one arm against the wall, so that Rugg could see the faces and backs of both of them at once. The bright brass swirls on the crown of Jadeen's head, Hilary's frown bent down at her and one eyebrow so far cocked that it was visible above the hornrims, Jadeen staring up overhead with her bottom lip drawn in and her tongue running along it, then the back of Hilary's head with his mother's strange thatch hair combed neatly down into the freckles on his nape. They were sure to have blond children.

"This corner of it isn't," he was saying. He took his arm down and wrapped his index finger in a white handkerchief. He looked, Rugg thought, more insouciant than ever in his concentration. He had the most unspeakably offhand way of looking at Jadeen. The very angle of his stance expressed that she was a not-too-bad chick that he might consider for his Saturday lay. The only thing more incomprehensible than this was that Jadeen responded to it—not to Hilary in spite of

80

it but to it, the attitude itself—with sideway looks (only not now, because now she was looking up overhead) through her lashes and quick little slides of her focus both saucy and servile.

"What's the trouble?" Rugg asked and both of them jumped and turned towards him, Hilary saying, "Lord," in general protest.

"Hello, Angus," Jadeen said. "I've got something in my eye, and Hilary's pretending it's ash, which it isn't. In September! It's lint off that silly bootie hanging in the car that some woman prob'ly knitted him up north."

"Lord," Hilary said again.

"Well, come into the den and let me get it out," Rugg said. "The light's terrible here."

"I can get it out, Dad. It'd be out now if you hadn't come sneaking . . ."

"Not with the flat of your finger in a dirty handkerchief it wouldn't be, Hilary. Her eye'd be out more likely."

"For chrissake, Dad . . ."

"Hilar*eee*," Jadeen broke in. "He *is* the eye doctor."

Hilary threw up his hands in mock acquiescence, the handkerchief flipping at the mirror frame. "Oh, yes, lord, yes, aren't we lucky to have an eye doctor in the family. Anybody hasn't got an eye doctor in the family they probably just commit suicide whenever they get something in their eye."

"That'll do, Holden, honey," Jadeen said.

He looked slapped for a second, then pocketed the handkerchief and touched his forehead to her with a flourish meaning, "touché". He quit them abruptly and lounged off into the dining-room, calling with heavy affection, "Hello, Mom! Where's my fat and fecund mother?"

Jadeen bit her lower lip as she looked after him. The light

F   81 went out of her skin, tight over high cheekbones that were the crest of a wide, full heart ending at her chin. Whenever Rugg realized that Jadeen loved his son he felt flustered and confused, and he said defensively to himself, I love him too, I love him but he's my son and I can't imagine loving him apart from wishing he were different. I don't see what it is in him that anybody else loves.

"Come on in here," he said. She followed him into the den and although, really, the light was fine as it was, he placed her busily under the strongest of the bulbs in the old candlesockets around the wall. The eye was red and watery from the irritation, and he held the lid down sideways for a second to force the tears towards the centre. The drop of water gathered just slightly muddy from having washed over a pencil line that was run fantastically around the eyelid *between* the roots of the lashes and the inner rim towards the eyeball. Seeing this, Rugg also saw that there were brown beads on Jadeen's lashes and at least two shades of green on her lids, which from two feet away you would not for an instant have suspected. Rugg thought, well, well.

He saw it at once when he stretched the lids apart: just an ordinary mote, probably ash, as a matter of fact.

"Umph." He took a piece of surgical gauze (a handkerchief would do as well, but certainly it ought to be a clean handkerchief), and folded a blunt corner into it. When he went for the mote Jadeen pulled her bottom lip in again and ran her tongue along it the same way she had before. It was a smallish tongue, rather pointed, the colour of poached salmon and as finely granulated as an Oregon pear. Rugg had an uncomplicated, consummately innocent desire to add his tongue to it just there where it reached the corner of her mouth. It was the most *isolated* impulse he had had all day, and his mind slid off

82

at the very edges of his imagination when he tried to see all the consequences it would have. There was something else, Rugg thought, that he would surely never do.

"That's got it."

She pulled the tongue in and closed her mouth on it, swallowed once and without thanking him first said, startingly, as if directly challenging his thought, "Angus, do you think anything is ever simple?"

"That's a pretty sweeping question, Jadeen. When you put it that way I guess I'd have to answer no."

"No. Well." She didn't move to leave, though, just stood looking up at him blinking the irritated eye and between blinks looking at him so hard that she probably wasn't seeing him.

"I mean, I've been wondering if there isn't *sometimes* something as plain as just wrong. Or just evil. As simple as my mother's kind of evil."

She licked her lip swiftly with the small pointed tip, wet as an Oregon pear, and that desire flushed all through Rugg again; not Desire, just the one specific desire to put his tongue there, and he thought, My God that's simple, the consequences wouldn't be but that's a simple thing.

"I don't mean what she thinks is evil, but I mean as *simple* as that. Angus, listen, when I was fifteen or so I began to understand that people had reasons for doing things, even the worst and ugliest things, and I began to believe that if we could ever know *all* the reasons for anything we'd *always* find it forgivable. I thought learning that meant I'd grown up. Now I'm not sure. I think I believe in bad. Most reasons are rationalizations, aren't they? If we accept reasons we have to accept Freud's reasons, or other ones even more knobbly and obscure, right on back to original sin. Then there'll be no

83

responsibility, will there? Even believing that 'bad' and 'evil' are arbitrary terms becomes a licence to perform them, doesn't it. Doesn't it, Angus?"

Allowing himself this much, he put his arm around her and walked her towards the dining-room and, thinking now of giving Mama Lily ten dollars, thinking of de Sevres, thinking of making Maeve cry for joy, he said, "A thing can be good or bad, can't it, Jadeen, without having to be simply so?"

But that wasn't what she meant, or wasn't enough of it, because even after she had kissed Maeve and told her to sit down, had gone out after the napkins that Maeve had forgotten and brought in the plates with the hot red crabs and the salad and the bowl of steaming sweetcorn, she turned to him, shutting out Hilary across the table by leaning her forehead on her hand between them, and said, "But your profession, for example, wanting to save eyes. Isn't that simply and entirely and self-evidently good? Isn't that good to want, good to learn, and good to do? Isn't it?"

Rugg cracked into the white belly of his first crab and scooped the lungs aside. It was no lie that he was tired, and tonight he either had to tell the whole thing in outline or else the penicillin part in detail, and before that decide which, so that he might just have said "I hope so, Jadeen," or even just "Yes," if Hilary hadn't laughed then in a way too consciously fond and familial and said, "Lord, now you've done it. I'll have to hear *two* lectures tonight."

So, ignoring this, although because of it, he said, "You'd think so, wouldn't you, Jadeen, and yet there was a time in France when the greatest optical surgeon in the world was prevented by law from figuring out an important way to do it, because it was considered immoral to take a piece of cornea the diameter of an extra fine pea out of an unclaimed corpse."

84

"There," Jadeen said, but with wavering certainty, "that's what I mean. If there was such a law it was simply and self-evidently bad then, wasn't it?"

"Maybe," Rugg replied. Hilary cracked a crab claw savagely. "But then does that mean the doctors who stole the corpses anyway were right?"

She made a shuddery face. "I see, I guess it doesn't."

"In any case it wasn't very efficient. Eye surgeons have never been particularly well organized for stealing two-hour-old corpses, and the eyes had to be no older, no deader than that when you grafted on to the living eye. Now, you see, we can preserve the corneas in penicillin for a couple of days, but in the early forties nobody was paying much attention to penicillin—it'd been discovered but not *discovered* if you see what I mean—and the eyes had got to be fresh."

"Couldn't you preserve them in alcohol?" Jadeen asked, and before Rugg could answer Hilary jumped in with Rugg's own most facetious lectern voice, "That would preserve them like a pickle, you see, madame, but it would also pickle them like a preserve. No, they'd got to be alive all right, and penicillin, you see, had been discovered, like a discovery, but not *discovered*, like a Hollywood starlet."

Maeve pouted at him warningly. Jadeen laughed and Rugg did too, thinking, I've been hated a lot in my life, I don't mind that, but nobody ever had so little regard for me as Hilary. Why is my son the only man I know who thinks me ridiculous? It isn't familiarity, Maeve's lived with me longer than he has, and even when she's furious with me it's fury, not contempt.

He said, "Luckily, you see, there was a war; and luckily for me we fought on the French side."

That, already, shocked Jadeen. She gathered her attention

85

entirely to him and stopped chewing her corn, one kernel balancing for a second on her lip before she sucked it in.

"The greatest eye surgeon in the world at the time was a man named Guillaume de Sevres. He'd been stealing fresh dead Parisian hoboes, *very* inefficiently, for several years; but when the Germans started to get pushed out of France he had a better idea. He just volunteered his services for *la gloire de France*, figuring that if there was any place a man could find enough cadavres, it ought to be in a hospital on the front."

Hilary opened his mouth for some comment from which Rugg found himself wincing before it came out. But Jadeen said, "I see," in a purposely bland, schoolteacher voice, and Hilary said nothing after all.

"Only, you see, that was just as inefficient of him as the other, because of course at the front they had other organs than eyes to patch up, and de Sevres was too big a man to send there anyway. They made some fine speeches at him and decorated him just for volunteering and put him in charge of optics at the Allied hospital back at Reuzarne.

"Now Reuzarne was pretty much the thing in those days. It had the biggest P.O.W. camp on French soil, and the hospital had all American equipment and about three-quarters of the wounded big brass on our side of the squabble. I was already there for eyes, and the only patient I'd seen below a captain was a count. Beautifully organized place, which was of course exactly what de Sevres didn't want. But there was one thing working in his favour."

"What?" Jadeen asked instantly, and Hilary shot her, now, a look of contempt, as if for encouraging a bore. Of all the snotty adolescent gall!

"Your real military man feels castrated in a hospital," Rugg replied loudly. "On the front an officer has to worry about the

86

shelling he's getting, and how not to. But a convalescent has nothing to worry about except the hypothetical future, and he's got to make it spectacular for himself so he doesn't get to feeling useless. All recuperating officers are expert tacticians, you can take my word for it. At Reuzarne the big topics were bacteria and poison gas.

"So one day every specialist in the place got a mimeographed order to 'inform' himself—they didn't say how—of the effects of germs and gasses on 'his' part of the body. And then, I think it said to, 'design preventative and curative measures'. You know, bandaids for streptococci and antidotes for cyanide. I remember the nose and throat man sent 'em a report recommending a certain brand of cough drops. The thing was generally scoffed at, which was all the better for de Sevres when he appeared to take it seriously.

"Yes, de Sevres said, he thought he could repair a gas-damaged cornea—and for all he knew or they knew, gas would damage corneas—but he'd have to have absolute control of his experiments and all the secrecy he felt he needed. And they gave it to him. That was the greatest miracle of the whole business, really, but de Sevres was grand at that kind of thing. Huge man, looked at you as directly as if he meant something in particular by it, which he seldom did. He could tell you his dog had fleas in such technical gobbledygook you'd think the fate of the race depended on it.

"So they gave it to him, his free hand. And then, you see, he was no longer so interested in thievable corpses. He had the finest equipment in the world, an international staff ditto, *military* authority such as a medical man can't hardly expect to get; he had me, and he had . . ."

Rugg checked Hilary sideways to see if he was going to spoil this pause, but Hilary was looking at his plate, making fork circles in his mayonnaise and perhaps—who could tell? —perhaps even listening a little, even listening as he used to when he was ten and twelve.

"And he had?" Jadeen prompted.

"He had twenty-two thousand German prisoners of war."

Jadeen frowned, part apprehensive, part incredulous. Maeve began unobtrusively clearing the table and, there, you could tell that *she* was following, as one follows a familiar song, not needing to hear the words but not wanting anything else to get in the way of them either.

"He didn't kill prisoners," Jadeen stated as a fact. "I won't believe you if you say he did."

"Certainly he didn't. He didn't need corpses because they were dead, Jadeen. He needed them because their eyes were still alive."

"Oh," Jadeen said, and looked away from him.

"That wouldn't have served any purpose at all, you see. He didn't only need an eye to get a cornea out of, he needed one to put it into too. Of course he didn't tell that to the military. He just said no questions could be asked about what became of the prisoners, and—hell, they were Germans—the brass looked wise and said that was all right with them.

"In fact what we had to do was offer the prisoners a really tempting reward. They had to be volunteers or we'd hardly learn anything at all. You can tell whether a man can *see* without his co-operation, but you can't tell whether he sees better with this lens than with that one, or on this side than the other, or whether he's got a headache, and where."

"And what did you offer them?"

"Oh, freedom. We didn't have anything else they wanted. That's where my part began, and that wasn't easy either, I

88

can tell you. The prisoners were a lot warier than the post commanders. They had no reason in the world to believe me, and they quite naturally assumed that once we got them in the operating room we were just going to carve them up from one end to the other."

"Quite naturally," Jadeen said with distaste.

"After a solid month I had only one man willing to take a chance on us. A shoe salesman from Cologne, he was. We'd rather have had two, but we didn't dare give him a chance to change his mind; so de Sevres and I went at him one after the other. De Sevres took a disc direct out of the centre of the right cornea, and then he stood aside holding it on a glass plate in his hand while I took the same size slice out of the left eye, but off centre. Then I stood aside and de Sevres sewed his graft into my eye, and then he sat down and I sewed mine into his. Whole thing took about half an hour."

"And what happened to the man?"

"He went blind, of course. Our tools were still quite crude in those days. It was the first time de Sevres had ever lifted a living graft, and it's the first time I'd ever done any of it on a human. But we managed to smuggle him into Switzerland, and from what I understand he got along all right. The fantastic thing was that somehow the prisoners found out about it; that we'd really got him into Switzerland, I mean. There are more kinds of wireless than one in a war. That's the second miracle if you like. After that, of course, we could hardly keep track of the volunteers. When we got the basic problems solved we'd work on two prisoners simultaneously, one eye each so nobody'd go entirely blind. That's the tiredest I've ever been in my life. We were fighting time, you see. We couldn't ever know when the war might end."

"I think that's disgusting!" Jadeen burst out. Rugg was

89

surprised. He often told students things like, "Luckily there was a war," because indignation was a form of attention. But he wouldn't have expected Jadeen to be so vehement.

"I've never heard such an inhuman story!"

"Oh, Jadeen, come on," Rugg said. "You hear more inhuman stories than that in this town every Saturday night."

"You were using them as guinea pigs!"

"Well, of course, Jadeen. Anybody who submits to a new operation is a guinea pig. A lot of people have died that way. We didn't even kill anybody."

He smiled at her. She put down her glass and gave him a fierce glare in exchange, the heart shape of her lower face destroyed by the way she clamped her jaw.

"That's exactly the same as they did at Dachau and Auschwitz!"

Hilary looked up at her and his forehead furrowed. Maeve stopped mid-turn with the catsup bottle, which swung from her hand like a pendulum. Rugg let out a breath, sat back in his chair and looked at Jadeen. She meant it. Well. It's because the young know all about that war now except what it was like to live in it, with it. It's because after an absolute war you apply absolute condemnations. Anybody who said "kike" in Pittsburgh in the thirties was guilty, now, for the atrocities in Poland. You propound an idea like collective guilt and sooner or later you find yourself comfortable with it: all men are equal, all men are guilty; ergo, all men are equally guilty. You've expunged the human factor as neatly as the Nazis expunged it from the idea of Jewry.

He said, "Not. At. All."

"I'd like you to explain to me how it's different!"

"All right, Jadeen. In the first place the patients were volunteers. In the second place we actually did give them the freedom we'd promised. And in the third place de Sevres was right about the eye. It is possible to patch an imperfect cornea with a piece of a perfect one. We spoiled twenty-four live eyes between us, de Sevres and I. I've saved sixteen hundred or so by now. You show me a Dachau doctor who made some contribution to medicine, Jadeen, before you start talking to me about Dachau."

Jadeen was silent. Hilary roused himself out of his chair, and saying "You oversimplify, Jadeen," took the cob dish out to the kitchen. Maeve said, "Come whip the cream for me, will you honey? While I make coffee, or Angus'll be late." Jadeen followed her frowning, passing through the swinging door Hilary held for her without looking up at him. Hilary came back to the table and that left the two of them there for several minutes, silent, Hilary sitting sideways with his arms hung over the chair back and his eyes on a bald spot his own feet had been wearing in the carpet ever since his legs reached that far. How is it possible, Rugg thought, to experience an awkward silence with somebody you've lived with for twenty years? You defended me just now, Hilary. Did you do it out of some obscure uncontrollable impulse to defend me, or to make your point with Jadeen? Whatever it was. Something she thought "simply wrong" so it had to do with sex; a pity and a shame the way these southern girls were raised.

"I understand there was some picket fighting at the docks this afternoon," he said.

"So I understand."

"You don't know anything more about it?"

"No."

"Will you be going down there?"

"No, Dad, I'm covering your speech."

That was all. He obviously minded covering it, but that

didn't hurt Rugg, what hurt was his not bringing the minding out in the open. Rugg didn't think much of Hilary's newspaper, Hilary wasn't required to think much of his speeches. It would be so easy for them to make a friendly joke of it: I guess you could just about write your story without going if I gave you the title. But he knew what Hilary would answer: that's right. And the smile would be polite at best. Then they would be back in the middle of this silence and all that effort wasted.

So Rugg decided not to throw any more pebbles into it, and they sat each looking as if he would not want his thoughts disturbed, each brooding about the other. The voices became gradually warmer and louder in the kitchen and finally broke into laughter, Jadeen's laugh beginning in a high girl's giggle and descending until it was full in her throat. That was the work of Maeve. Miracle Maeve. She could not wash six glasses without breaking one, she was always late and unkempt and out at elbows, but she could put people back together with a few words and touches. Even Hilary, who seemed to hate everything in the world except welfare projects and the city room, even he saw the feminine, unclever miraculousness of his mother. That was something they could share if Hilary would let it happen.

They came through the swinging door, Jadeen with the shortcake tray shouldering it back and holding it for Maeve, who brought the coffee. They exchanged a smile as they passed, full of some mysterious bond. Mysterious because they had no bonds really, not age or blood or experience or goal. And not really pregnancy either because Maeve had had that and was having it and for Jadeen it was still an idea for the uncertain future. But that was it, the idea of pregnancy, which could make a bond between any arbitrary two women

92

in the world, as no single thing could be said to bind every two men.

"So I decided on the yellow after all," Maeve said, "because it's such a nuisance having to explain to people that you *like* blue for little girls. Yellow's nice anyway. Come up and see it after coffee if you have time."

"Will I, Hilary?" Jadeen asked and dropped a kiss on his neck at the base of his ear, going directly on to Maeve without waiting for an answer, "And did you get the crib done?"

"Yes," Maeve answered, then stopped with the pot mid-air so that the stream of coffee wavered and sloshed over the cup rim, "that is no, I . . ."

"I closed the paint can, dear," Rugg said.

"Did you Angus? That was sweet of you."

"Who was it?"

"Who was what?"

"On the telephone. Didn't the telephone ring?"

"Oh, I see. No. No, as a matter of fact I thought of something Hilary used to have, some silver bells on a bar, and I thought I knew right where to lay my hands on it. But I didn't after all, and then I lost track of the time looking through his school things, and his things before that. There was the loveliest little pair of white wool training pants, but horribly stained; I don't think they can even be dyed. Angus, do you remember the time I had to take papa to the doctor before you got home and left Hilary in the playpen and . . .?"

"Do I!" said Rugg. "I came in, Jadeen, his mother probably hadn't been gone seven minutes, and there he was flipped over and pivoting around on his belly in the most impressive quantity of babyshit you ever hope to see. Bright yellow stuff.

93

I didn't know which end to pick him up by. Oh, Hilary, for God's sake don't look *embarrassed*, that wasn't you, it was a little baby you didn't even know. Jadeen's no prude, are you, Jadeen?"

"I think it's sweet," Jadeen said.

Hilary shrugged and shoved his dessert away. Maeve spread her whipped cream even over the shortcake with the back of her spoon and licked the spoon with the bowl upside down. She smiled, at Jadeen again, not at them, and said, to Jadeen, "I remembered so much going through those boxes this afternoon, things I didn't remember remembering. It's strange about growing older, you keep being mainly astonished that you don't feel older, you don't feel thirty, you don't feel thirty-five, you're forty and you don't believe it. Sometimes I see a man and think, there's an attractive boy, and it turns out he's fifty-five. That catches me up, you know."

"*Do* you now," Rugg said.

"But this afternoon I was pure twenty again for an hour or so, and it *is* different. Oh, I'd never have thought of that time again if it hadn't been going to happen again. Isn't that strange? And yet it's the thing in my life that's been the most worth thinking about. All I've had left of it is a kind of vague interest in other people's newborn babies, and I'd forgotten why."

Hilary pushed his cup across and asked, "Coffee?" in an oddly loud voice, as if somehow he really could be embarrassed by this talk, a boy who grew up in a medical family and could have drawn you a diagram of the reproductive organs when he was five. Rugg couldn't figure him out. Maeve filled the cup and chattered, to Jadeen.

"We were very big on Freud in the forties, Angus and I, and I remember that one day when I was bathing Hilary, I

94

was soaping his little pink bottom cheeks—he'd been clean a long time, you know, but I was just standing there silly-happy feeling the soap slip over him—and I thought of Freud and I just burst out laughing. I couldn't understand why nobody'd told him to mind his own business, pompous old thing. I was simply in love with my son, it wasn't the least bit different from being in love with anyone else."

Jadeen pressed her hands hard together between her knees and drew one breath of pleasure at this. Hilary made a wry face and stirred his coffee in an elaborate olde-worlde way.

"He used to have awful colic in the mornings; I'd forgotten that until this afternoon. After I fed him at four in the morning he'd scream with pain and anger, sometimes two hours while the sun came up and the birds went screeching around the back trees. The birds were mad that year. Hilary and I would walk on the porch, he screaming and me crying silently and the birds just yelling at us. Oh, it was awful, but it was my best time.

"When the sun was high enough to warm the porch I'd put him in the swing where his eyes were out of the light but the rest of him was in it, and then I'd take off all his clothes and just look at him and stroke him till he began to feel the sun. There's nothing you can love like flesh, is there? He'd calm down, then, only crying in snatches, and I'd start kissing him at his hands or nibbling the soles of his feet. He was irritated at first, and would bat at me or pull away, but after a while he lay still and then began to coo, a soft laugh sound in his throat while I went systematically down the outside of his arm and up the inside, down his chest to the deep white hollow just before his thigh, kissing him all over, simply in love with him, totally and entirely and sensually in love with him."

95

She stopped. She and Jadeen shared their smile, in the eyes alone this time. Rugg looked at Maeve, her pied face balanced breathless on her long neck, and he thought, Jesus, yes, that blue: sea blue, day blue, the colour of space.

"Luckily," Hilary said, "I don't remember any of it."

Eight o'clock, Jadeen

In the car she kissed him and asked, "All better?" and he said yes and smiled. But it wasn't. It was smoothed over the top and tangled underneath like the hairdo of a high school queen. When he dropped her he only called, "McPhay at nine!" and the car shot from her in one screech of angry fleeing, taking the blind corner without a pause. This left her so abruptly, so cut off, on the sidewalk at her mother's gate, that confusion and panic suddenly threatened her. She hadn't been here for six weeks, not since the day she finally and definitely said she was going to marry Hilary. The sun had gone down while they were at dinner, making it hotter by the paradox, sheer contrariness, of its not being any cooler. The smell of honeysuckle like a sticky liquid flowed out from her mother's courtyard, cloying, trapping.

This was Noon Street, the next parallel to McPhay in the core of the old quarter, more fashionable even than McPhay for shopping, and everything stayed open till ten in the tourist season. So there were too many faces to keep track of and she had to go in or risk meeting somebody she knew, Mr. Terrance in his wicker chair in the antique shop or Mrs. Jarris who would tell her how hadn't she grown! how blonder! how to be proud of! She got out her key, but she still didn't go in for a minute. She looked at the antiques and tried to find their ugly familiarity reassuring, measuring out the size of this rectangle of Noon between Rubins and Sampler Streets, the streets she had not been allowed to cross when she was eight and they moved back here. She had so cut herself off from this place, had begun it so long ago even before she went away from it, that she always forgot how it made her feel to find herself in it all of a sudden. She *always* forgot, the way she always forgot that Narses replaced Belisaurus as Justinian's general, which kept coming up on history quizzes and which she never mastered until she'd got a B minus and lost her chance at Phi Bet. When she was away from it she said, "my mother's place", as if it was in another city, all the way west or in some no-land with thick fog-banks around it. Even when she was still in high school she'd begun putting distance between herself and it so that as long as she was outside the boundaries of Rubins and Sampler she lived in a white bungalow on the university side of the outskirts and had a father and a dog. She didn't lie about it but she behaved that way. She had trained her mind so well that when she came home from State and Hilary said, as if it was a new upsetting idea, "You're going to get an apartment by yourself?" she thought, what does he mean, what else would I get, with whom would I share it? They hadn't been engaged then or she might not have got it, they might just have got married instead. Now they had a place to be, so they had time not to be married, to walk lovers in flat shoes in the alleys with their bare arms tangled and the old musicians clucking at them the way they never would if they were married. They were both working and saving and they were going to go to Europe for their honeymoon, Paris for her and Spain for him, and they talked about hopping a cattle boat to Greece or Africa; they knew somebody who'd done it.

Thinking of that helped. Her mother was a long long ways from Greece. Jadeen smiled, but still taking a deep breath through the smile, and unlocked the courtyard gate, giving two warning rings on the brass bell. The carriageway was dank and inside the court it was even closer, hotter than in the street, like a pocket of abrupt jungle. The banana tree was choked with perfumy parasitic vines that grew then around the second-story balustrade with the speed of slow worms crawling. They were always hacked back in the fall but it hadn't been done yet; the vines had run out of climbing space and had begun to drop, looping down the mezzanine supports and reaching out for a way back up that wasn't there. You could hardly find a handhold on the stair rail, and you needed it because Mommy (she was almost there now and "my mother" was gone) was having the splintery stairs just naturally scrubbed away. They were scrubbed every morning even though nobody went up them most days but the woman to scrub them, and they hadn't been repaired since Jadeen was eight and used to sit on them picking little balls like rubber cement out of her nose, missing her father and the other side of the river and pretending that she was Margaret O'Brien missing her father and the other side of the river.

"Ger-al-*dine*?"

Mommy called as usual, making the name long and royal, but she didn't come out as usual with her suffocating hug. Well, all right. Jadeen was willing to let her define it. If the atmosphere was to be cool, so much the better, very much better than that last scene with its exasperating mixture of Christianity and family pride. Jadeen said she was going to marry Hilary and Mommy said she was going to leave the house to the historical society, humiliating both of them not because Jadeen was being disowned but because Mommy didn't have anything really fine to disown her from. In the act, the pose of disinheriting, she had been frailer and more pitiful than Jadeen had ever seen her, and it was that sight,

99

not the anger, she'd been keeping away from these six weeks. God help them if the historical society turned it down, then she'd have to pretend to beg forgiveness to save Mommy's face.

"Geraldine, is that you? Come in, then. Don't stand out in the . . . *cold*, ahaha, child!"

The French doors opened directly into the big parlour, at its best like this in the last twilight just before you absolutely had to put the lights on, when you could see the glow and plush of everything but not the scratches and worn spots. The walls were covered with something that wasn't cut velvet but could pass for it, the colour that was called plum but was really much redder than a plum. The legs of everything were as graceful as a spider's legs and the tapestry footstools had gold claws. There was a crystal chandelier over the baby grand, converted to electric but never lit; a table made all of crystal, even the legs, with a snowstorm in a globe on it and a fish carved out of jade with a watch for an eye. Every surface, of the fireplace that had no flue, the piano that nobody played, the glass case they'd lost the key to, every surface was the excuse for a knick-knack, expensive useless things, some of them beautiful, all of them curious. It was a room that you couldn't be at home in, woman or girl, if you were anything like Jadeen, but that you could be attached to. If it was your favourite aunt's parlour that you had played in on Sundays when you were a little girl you'd be terribly fond of it. She'd had too much of it, that's all. She'd wanted a dog for week-days.

Mommy hadn't got up from the divan, and her spine was straight as righteousness, but she arched her head to invite a kiss if Jadeen would come to *her*, saying, "Gracious, there you are, you naughty girl, such a long time without coming to see

100

your poor old mother." She laughed gaily. Jadeen, surprised and relieved that it was to be the gaiety instead of the coldness or the woundedness, went to Mommy and took her hand and brushed her lips in the hollow of the cheek. Mommy smelled of dry-sachet and plain unperfumed cologne. Her hair was combed straight upwards all around from the roots and piled in four or five curls on top the way people wore their hair in the forties, old-fashioned but not old-fashioned enough to go with the furniture.

"There's been so much to do getting used to school," Jadeen said vaguely, and Mommy took this up instantly, so eager to excuse her that it made Jadeen wince.

"Well, good land, of course there has, think of my baby! Teaching school. Bridget's been telling me just how fine you're doing."

Before she finished saying this, Jadeen had become aware, by that means that is clearly sensual and yet does not attach itself to any of the senses in particular, that there was a third person in the room. Turning, she saw Bridget Honeywell in the highest of the wing-back chairs, the chair all grace and flight and glow, The Bridge still tight and square in the grey linen suit and fingering her shingled neck in embarrassment.

"Hello, Jadeen, I didn't think . . ." she said, plainly about to say, "I didn't think you'd come," but stopping before that and, dropping her arms on the arched chair arms to deny that she felt ill at ease, saying instead, "I'm very pleased to see you here."

"Yes," Jadeen said. She looked at The Bridge for a minute. and put her bag down, not sitting.

"Well, now," Mommy said, "sakes, go out in the kitchen and see what you can rustle up, not that there's a lot, an old lady living alone, but some cornbread surely and a compote of apple and blackberry just this week. Some port wine for Miss Honeywell, not, Bridget? Well, we always say 'rustle up' because Uncle Dan the old captain, God rest him, after he'd been west it got into the family. Geraldine?"

"I've just eaten, Mommy. But I'll get the wine if you like."

"I, not I, well!" smiling and rolling her eyes at Miss Honeywell. "I've never been the *drinking* branch of the family!—but you know that from the old days, don't you, Bridget? The times we had, girls together! Geraldine? Compote and cornbread surely, in the fridge, not the cornbread of course. Bridget, don't you think she's looking thin? You do work them, that I know. A slaver, now, isn't she, Geraldine, isn't she?"

"I'm not any thinner, Mommy."

She went out to the kitchen where the black and white harlequin floor tiles were as warped as a piece of solidified sea, Mommy's voice following her shrill in the semi-dark, "I can remember the time, Bridget, when she was plump as a gooseberry, plump as an apple's cheek, say! You wouldn't believe it except of course you remember too don't you, here I'm forgetting. Well I never for the *life* of me where she got it because I was always slender myself, too slender really, old Uncle Dan used to put his two hands round my waist and touch fingers, so. I'm not saying his hands weren't large!"

Jadeen took out the pot of apple and blackberry—when she opened the old fridge door she heard the mice feet scuttle underneath into the baseboard—and cut two slices of the crumbly cornbread, scraping the crumbs up with the side of her hand and then at the last minute shoving them off on to the floor towards where the mice had gone. God damn The Bridge, what made her come here, what good was that supposed to do? Did she think she'd have to *win* Mommy over to her side? Coming here was the first thing to make Jadeen feel like a little girl and have to go through with it even if she decided she didn't want to. She wasn't going to decide that, but even if she did. Why was The Bridge so stupid when she wasn't stupid really? And now Mommy was half hysterical just with having a visitor. Of course, Miss Honeywell couldn't have expected that, but then on the other hand if she'd bother to come and see Mommy sometimes when she didn't want anything of her then she might know how lonely Mommy was and how nervous she got when somebody finally came to see her. Thinking this, Jadeen remembered that she had not been here for six weeks, and she slammed the bread-box.

"And her father just about average although he might have got stout later in life, that's something I'll never know. Ah, me, God bless him. Anyhow I said to myself, wherever did I get such a puh-*lump* little pickaninny, hanh?"

Mommy's high laughter fidgeted about the house. Jadeen put the port, glasses, compote, bread, on a tray. She would eat a piece of bread and jam and drink no port, she decided, just contrary to her inclination, because the trick was not to fight the little things. That's the way she'd got through that many years with Mommy, and that's the way she'd saved up for the big breaks, college and her apartment and Hilary. If she ate some bread and drank no wine it would keep it in front of her and she wouldn't get excited.

"Weren't you, Geraldine?" Mommy said as she came back. "I was just telling Bridget how plump you used to be, do you remember, honey?"

"Well, yes, Mommy," Jadeen said setting down her tray. "Miss Honeywell had me in her English classes when I was fat. She remembers."

"Well, of co-ourse! she does, aren't I getting silly in my old age now. Not fat, Geraldine, I wouldn't say fat. But do you remember how plump she was, Bridget? No wine for me, Geraldine, but you go right on ahead if you like, dear, I know young people."

The Bridge accepted a glass of port and said, "Thank you, Jadeen," quietly, and something happened to her face that Jadeen had never seen happen to it before. It lost its hardness in a smile of frank apology, confession. Her eyebrows relaxed and the line of her jaw softened, and Jadeen thought that this was perhaps the first moment they had shared as individual people, and thought how suddenly feminine Miss Honey-well's face was, and thought for a brief instant before the smile passed, why should defeat make her face more feminine, why is defeat feminine?

But she'd made her decision, so she sat down without smiling back and said, "No, Mommy, I'll just have some of your good compote." The Bridge sipped her wine, her brows knitted up and on different levels again, not knowing if she'd been rebuffed or not. Mommy arched her neck like a cat being stroked and said, "Just as you like dear, but not for my sake *please.*"

"WELL," Mommy said when The Bridge had her wine and Jadeen had her bread and sauce and Mommy, seeing that these things had been taken care of, had leaned back into the divan and spread the emptiness of her own hands out on either side of her. There was a great pause like the arching of a sea wave, everybody standing and watching it as the under-tow backs farther and farther into the roll of smooth water and the wave leans over the sea in a great pause before the foam breaks at the top and Mommy said, "Well. What's this I hear now, Geraldine, Bridget tells me you're having a little bit of trouble over one of the textbooks. Didn't you want to teach out of it, honey?"

Not to let the wave tumble and roar, holding it back with main strength and not looking at either of them, Jadeen chewed and swallowed her whole mouthful. The compote was delicious even after a full meal, mellow and tart. Mommy was a better cook than Maeve; nobody had anything to show the South about food.

"I don't think the book is a good model in composition for my students, Mommy," she said then.

"Well, but goodness, Geraldine, wasn't it the Board that chose it, I mean didn't they approve it? You have to be humble and not uppity, honey, why those people have been in the school business for years now—isn't that right, Bridget? —and surely they must *know*, mustn't they? Why, Geraldine, Dr. Evardin is on the School Board, you must remember Dr. Evardin, Geraldine. When you had your tonsillitis?"

Jadeen said nothing to this but, "Yes, I do," eating and letting Miss Honeywell tap uncomfortably on the stem of her goblet. She didn't know how far Mommy and Miss Honeywell had got in their discussion but she was not going to offer them anything; they could let her know however they chose, and after a bit Mommy visibly chose to do it. She sat up straight again with a little roll of her back like shouldering responsibility and set her hands palm up in her lap, one on the other.

"The Nigras, Geraldine," she said. Mommy pronounced this word as if the Negroes in question were really niggers and she was too polite to say so. It sat there in the air all alone like a title or a précis, or maybe it was meant to be the whole argument, Jadeen hoped to God it was. It told them all they needed to know anyway: that Miss Honeywell had explained about *Race and the Human Race*, what it was about and why Jadeen didn't want to teach it; which side Mommy was on and what kind of tone she was going to take to say so. Agree with everything and leave, she told herself, agree with everything and go out and meet Hilary, it's twenty after eight, there's only forty minutes to hold on and be Geraldine.

"Well, honey, you know very well yourself how I feel, I feel that all men are brothers under God, but we're only human and we've got to have limits don't you see, Geraldine. You know yourself that I braved the wrath of your Aunt Cassy and went down for years, for *years* until these migraines started, and gave bible class every Sunday night at the Nigra Institute. And Aunt Cassy and Cousin Peter cursed me and reviled me; isn't that so, Geraldine?"

Well, it was so. No matter what you thought of the bible classes, she'd stood up to Aunt Cassy's nastiness to do it and that must have been harder than standing up to Mommy.

"Yes, that's so."

Mommy sighed, a real sigh from the time when women really sighed. "Well then, Geraldine, I can assure you that I know whereof I speak, honey. And I know that young people nowadays are not so *sensitive* to a number of things as we used to be. Odours for instance. It's because the city has come crowding in on us here and the air isn't pure—even the lake, Geraldine, you should have smelled how pure the lake was when I was a girl—but it's just a fact that the nigras have an odour that is particularly and peculiarly their *own*. I do assure you. Now I know that there have been very scientific attempts to prove a lot of biological things and so forth but really Geraldine some things are evident and I have to tell you that the nigras *do smell*. Now haven't you noticed that, Geraldine?"

Miss Honeywell stirred in her chair and said hesitantly,
106

"Carlotta, I hardly think . . ." and Jadeen looked up quickly at her wretched face and thought, no, you hardly think that is the kind of argument to use on Geraldine Spatch, Rotating Supply, Miss Honeywell; because you do not know anything. You do not know that these silly sentences climb through the spaces in my logic like the vines on the balustrade because I was brought up to believe this and there at the bottom of my beliefs that belief remains as small and as insistent as the pea of the real princess under the mattresses. You do not know that the last time my father took me to Joyland Park on the bay and I got lost from him in the midway crowd a gigantic Negro sailor without any shirt on swung me up to carry me back to him, and that I was so shocked, terrified by the acrid all-enveloping game-meat stink of his bare chest against my face that I could not cry and I cannot now, I cannot even now without a great firm wilful effort of my mind realize that he did something kind for me.

"Now sometimes, Geraldine, honey," Mommy said in the sort of voice that is so sweet you have to slap something, and Jadeen braced her buttocks against the voice and the words both, "sometimes we get used to a common and familiar sight and we no longer look at it afresh, like the shacks down the other side of Whalley. You must know it breaks my heart to say it, but the nigras have no pride."

It was really too far into twilight even for this room now, it was no longer dim, it was getting dark. Thirty-five more minutes, agree with everything, I wonder if it would upset her if I put a light on, the farthest one wouldn't show up anything, Jadeen thought and squeezed a piece of cornbread.

"No *pride*," Mommy repeated. "You walk down our own Rubins Street, now you know this is true, and you see the loveliest cared-for patios, and you just cross Whalley Avenue,

107

you just cross it! Think now, isn't that so, the weeds in all the cracks and things not painted and the *bugs*, Geraldine, they don't even fight the bugs! It breaks my heart."

Jadeen scooped her thumb hard into a groove on her chair arm. "They have no D.D.T. because they can't pay for it, and they have no pride because we've stolen it away from them bit by bit." She had meant not to say that sort of thing, and now she had said it it was wrong for the wrong reason. It was wrong because it fit, it could have slipped into Mommy's clichés unnoticed. Miss Honeywell's steady look said that to her, and Jadeen pressed her thighs all the tighter together thinking agree and go, agree and go. Mommy rose and paced round behind the sofa, her face suffused with a kind of unbearable benevolent patience.

"It's my fault, Bridget," she said sadly. "Well you try to do right by your children and instil good Christian practices in them and it's so hard to maintain a balance. We taught her to be charitable, even before her father died we began teaching her that, to give to those that were not so fortunate as she and . . ."

Mommy turned to Jadeen and Jadeen thought don't tell that story don't tell that story if you tell that story I'll, and Mommy said, "Why, Geraldine, now there's a thing you must remember, that shows you about the *violence*, honey, it's just inbred that's all. It's terribly sad but you can't deny it."

"Don't tell about that, Mommy," Jadeen said involuntarily aloud, wishing instantly that she had not; Mommy turned away and smiled her natively gentle smile and began fingering the ridges in a brass candlestick on the end table.

"Geraldine used to have a certain doll, Bridget, you know the way children are about certain toys, you can't see any rhyme or reason to it but that's the way they are, an ordinary

Betsy-Wetsy doll, I think her daddy brought it to her from a trip."

Wrong, wrong. It was a Kewpie doll, cheap bisque, seventeen inches high from the same carnival, the same last time at Joyland Park before daddy went away and didn't come back and they said much much later that he was dead. Or was killed. There was something odd about it because they mourned in such a strange qualified way, saying tsk tsk without grief, the way people mourn a suicide, but it wasn't suicide because then they wouldn't have got the insurance. To Jadeen it didn't matter anyway, he'd been dead ever since he left because even if she didn't distinguish clearly yet between dead and away she knew he wasn't coming back. She'd known it the night that was not her last sight of him but was her last memory of him now, when he took her to the Joyland Park midway. The big Negro brought her to him, she dumb with terror, and it was five minutes of daddy's coaxing before she could even burst into tears. Then he took her to the ring toss and told her anything she wanted, any any any thing at all she was to pick it and he would win it for her. She picked the doll. It had a purple net tutu with spangles and a silver wand, but those were gone by the time that Mommy was talking about.

"Well, it had sat in her closet for four or five years anyway without its ever coming out except at Christmastime when we got the old toys together to give away to the poor down the other side of Whalley. That was our way. Every year we did it. Well, Geraldine *never* played with that old doll but every single year she'd get it out and decide she couldn't part with it. Sweet really don't you think? Children have their ways."

"Mommy, Miss Honeywell doesn't want to hear this," Jadeen said tightly, trying not to say more because it would

109

only get worse. "It has nothing to do with what she came about."

"Why, Geraldine." Mommy turned a look of gentle astonishment on her; the folds of skin in her neck stretched taut. "Don't you see that it does? I'm simply saying that the nigras don't respect things, honey, and they've a certain violence about them. . . . *Racial* characteristics." She got the word "racial" out with difficulty, the way Jadeen got out "sixty-nine", something there was no really polite name for at all.

"Please, Mommy."

Miss Honeywell started to rise. Her napkin slid down her knees and she caught at it and Mommy raised her voice, "WELL," and somehow Miss Honeywell sat down again and Mommy made hard circles around the candlestick with her thumb and forefinger, one over the other up the length of it.

"Well, she must have been twelve or so when she finally decided to give up that ugly old doll. I'm not saying it was a nice doll, it wasn't, but it meant something special to her, because of her poor dead daddy you see. So we got in the car with the old toys box, Mizz Ambilene from the church school driving. We went right down into the *heart* of Nigra Town, stopping every house we saw any sign of children, and I got out and set something down inside the fence. Geraldine wasn't allowed to get out because of the bacteria—you never know do you—but she especially wanted to choose the place to give that doll and I told her she could do it herself if she'd set it down by the gate and run back right straight to the car."

"Mommy, Miss Honeywell doesn't want to hear this," Jadeen said. "I don't want to hear it."

Mommy smiled very sweetly at Jadeen and took the candlestick up, twisting it in her hands, and Jadeen said, "I'm going to leave," and Mommy went right on without paying her any mind, but her voice louder and half an octave up.

"We drove and drove and saw all sorts of little pickaninnies, Bridget, but they wouldn't do, oh no, not for my baby, she had to have the poorest little pickaninny in Pickaninny Town, mmm Geraldine? Well, and finally she found just the place that suited her, a little girl sitting in some mud by her steps just scrambling her little black fingers around in it—a *little* girl but I think she was older than Geraldine, she looked, you know . . . *developed*. Well, I was apprehensive but little Geraldine was as stubborn then as big Geraldine is now, Bridget, and it was to be *that* little girl or none. So she got out with the doll and went up to the fence and stood there and after a while the little nigra girl got up off her steps and come the other side of the gate. Well! Bridget, she had some awful kind of something, her eyes and her nose were running and running an awful clotted green stuff down her dirty face, it was crusted and scummy and runny and great scabs where she'd been picking at the crusty part and it running so. Oh, I can hardly bear to think! So scummy and the scabs, well, I ought to have gone and got Geraldine back right then but I tell you I was simply frozen!"

"That's enough, Mommy. Stop it," Jadeen said rising, and Mommy backed around the divan away from her, not looking at her but fending her off with the candlestick.

"Geraldine was frightened too, she won't say so now but I know it, Bridget, because of the way she pushed that doll all at once through the fence-pickets and when the little nigra girl took it by the leg she jumped back to the edge of the walk and stood stock still there. So I shouted, 'Geraldine! Geraldine!' and still she didn't come so I went out and ran over to her and by the time I got there do you know what happened? Do you know? That little scab-face pickaninny picked up a piece of garden hose laying there and she set that doll down in the dirt and she just naturally beat it and beat it and beat it . . ."

Mommy struck with the candlestick and it glanced off the wood with a dull whack. She raised the stick over her head and brought it down again; the sofa cushion let out an explosive gasp. Not like that at all, Jadeen thought, it was a splintering sound like nutshells in the cracker.

". . . until it broke into a million pieces," Mommy said.

Bridget Honeywell stood up and looked everywhere for a minute except at Mommy, who still had one end of the candlestick in her hand while the other end rose slowly and foolishly back up with the filling of the cushion.

"Jadeen," The Bridge said, "your mother is tired . . . I didn't realize. Your mother is overtired and anxious about you, Jadeen . . ."

The Bridge's face jumped into focus, the eyes round and shifting behind the glasses that had slipped down her nose, peering scared into the nearly dark room, and Jadeen thought again why in God's name did she come here, and she thought, I'm going to say something, I'm going to say something awful, it'll be too loud.

"Don't apologize for my mother," she said, shouted. "Don't you dare apologize to me for my mother!" And then, realizing that of all the possible things she might have said, shouted, this was the thing she had chosen, she snatched up her bag and ran from them, out the French doors and along the terrace and nearly down the steps till she felt her balance going and caught at a post and hung there with her face in the hot honeysuckle.

Her name was Quinella Price because that made Q.P. for initials, Kewpie, that was Daddy's joke. She splintered like nuts in the cracker and all the time the girl's great white-eyed black running face was turned towards Jadeen, not the doll, the white eyes saying I'm doing this on purpose, I'm doing it to shock you, I'm doing it because I hate you. And why, what for, thought Jadeen weeping. It wasn't my fault, I was as innocent as you. I understand now about condescension and contempt but I was born to it and taught to it the same as you were born and taught to hate. I'm to blame for the outgrown gloves and the unstrung rackets I gave away, but if you don't see the difference between those and Quinella Price, why should I be required to know the difference between pity and love? And now if I give up my job? My town? Hilary Rugg? And then if you take to my losses with a garden hose, how will I accept that?

She hung there in the silence and the sweet smell and the heat of the close courtyard and it was so still she heard Mommy's long heavy sigh above her and then through the French doors her voice limp and slow, not so much breaking the silence as wandering into and over it, "Well, Bridget, I don't know. I can't remember ever wanting any other thing than to be a good mother. Sometimes it seems to me there are lots of other people's children I could have been a good mother to. Sometimes I think that Geraldine wasn't really *meant* to be *my* daughter . . ."

Jadeen pulled her face from the vine and straightened her dress, taking care not to lean towards the creak at the middle of the step. She thought, ten to nine. Hilary.

"Well I'll tell you now," Mommy's voice came low and moaning from above, "I think of all those ovaries, Bridget, that came and went, came and went, came and went. Seems

H   113 like some kind of mix-up that Geraldine was the one that took. Blue-eyed ovaries, church-going ovaries, ovaries that liked to knit . . . I suppose it's a sin to regret your ovaries. Do you think so, Bridget? Do you think it is?"

Eight o'clock, Hilary

Hilary floorboarded full down Noon and around on to Sampler on two tyres without looking, then he braked with the same furious force and jolted squealing into an empty space not half a block out of sight of Jadeen at her mother's gate. That helped both take-off and landing. He accelerated hard again in neutral and pushed with all his strength against the steering wheel at straight-arm's length, his head finding the roof support through the padding.

He relaxed. The roar ran down into a smooth soft idling. He laid his arms around the wheel and slid his buttocks into the scoop of the bucket seat and he thanked his father for two things and two things only, the one unchosen sperm that had become himself and the out-of-character gift of an enclosed and private mobile space. He spread his arms out over the seat back and wrapped his car around him, thinking this is where I live, this is where I can be both alone and me, this is the only room I've ever had; and thinking that when his father got in the MG he looked confused and cumbersome, hunching his shoulders and twisting his knees this way and that and whipping the windows open saying "umph" and "ahh" and twitching his backside like a claustrophobic buffalo. Whereas he, Hilary, who was taller, folded down into it as easy as a letter in an envelope; in his father's Packard he felt thin and formal and absurdly high above the road.

He could spare ten minutes because they wouldn't start on time and he could find out who did the introduction from somebody else. He could actually have stayed away altogether if Rugg had offered to give him a summary, which of course he wouldn't because he couldn't bear to lose a member of his audience, and which of course if he had Hilary would have refused. Hilary was seized with a kind of furious frustration that bubbled and sloshed around in him while he sat dead calm with his arms draped backwards into the jump seat. He knew how he would spend these ten precious minutes of absolute silent solitude: saying My Problems Are Imaginary, like his father at *Snow White* when the witch-queen came on and little Hilary ran to the lobby, saying, "But, Hilary, it isn't *real*, it isn't *real*," trying hard to sound reasonable and not admit he was annoyed because he was missing part of the picture, "Don't you understand it isn't *real*?" And the trouble with that is that it always *is* real, everything is just as real as everything else. The film is real and the terror is real and somewhere is a real somebody who has studied up on just the mean, the average amount of fear to delight an average child, which will then inevitably leave some others indifferent popping their popcorn bags and some others weeping in the lobby with their fathers saying, "But it isn't *real*."

Now nothing in all the tumbled rummage of his mind was real except one job and, if he bungled it, one decision. He had to show Jadeen that she misinterpreted her duty, and if he couldn't he had to go north with her or else ask her to give up teaching and marry him. See? Simple. But imaginary things kept obscuring it, things as imaginary as dust on a camera lens. She held him responsible for puncturing her southern complacencies, and if he held her back now, wouldn't she always despise him just a little? How could he simply pick up and go north when he had made such an impassioned case for needing to be home and at work? And that? Had that been the maximum eighty-five per cent sincere of the best human motives, or had he been mainly afraid to leave Jadeen alone in this wolf-lair city for two winters? She'd said, "What a waste of a woman!" about his mother once, and he had agreed. "I never wanted to be her full-time job. Maybe dad did." Could he ask Jadeen to turn housewife for him? And supposing she said—always supposing she said no!—but also supposing she said yes. What happened to their idea of themselves then?— windswept youth on the top of a hill marching hand in hand towards the horizon, that Jadeen loved because she wanted so much to be good and fine and because it reminded her of some movie or other, and that Hilary loved because Jadeen in the midst of her most startling lapses, Rebecca quoting Norman Vincent Peale, was most Jadeen, Jadeen.

That ran under everything, as far under his packed hurting head as the sensation of a vacuum in his stomach, the fear of losing Jadeen, losing her in distance or in essence, and the weird thing was that the sensation was exactly the same as, and so kept cruelly reminding him of, that shock-sick moment of doubting joy when he realized that she was not pulling away or pretending it was a joke but was pressing her hard little belly in its damp red bathing-suit against his thigh and pulling strong on his neck as if she couldn't get far enough up into that kiss. Her hair was dripping on his hands and her shoulders had gone gooseflesh in a night breeze that sprang up out of the gulf. They were a little high from drinking sloe gin through straws out of a hollowed water-melon; everybody drank more than they wanted because it was sexy to be splayed out on the sand around the water-melon like spokes around a hub. And so he was high and dared her to the pier because she'd come with Royce Tellemens and was the prettiest girl there, and Suzanne his date was more interested in her guitar than him or gin *or* the sea. He raced her, winning so easily that he made a few circles around her on the way while she laughed and cantered. Finally she ran straight into the surf and when he chased her there she screamed and stumbled splashing out under the pier and he thought well, what the hell, and pinned her hard against the post and her mouth split like a ripe plum and for a second all his sensations were suspended in astonishment, the way the pain is delayed from a sharp-blade wound. Then a shudder went through her not from the breeze but from inside, the water lapped over their feet and he felt shock-sick with doubt and hope and desire. They broke breathing hard both of them from the running, so he exaggerated that not to look as if he were ashamed of breathing hard and, watching both himself and her from a slight distance not quite sure that he understood what was going on, thinking that maybe she had a different set of signals than other girls or maybe she was just a tart though he had never heard anyone say so, he leaned one hand on the pillar and said, experimenting, "Well, yes now, O.K. You'll do. I'm going to marry you. Jadeen, isn't it?" She laughed, scandalized, and started shivering; it was breezy but it wasn't that cold.

Jadeen loved to remember it. Whenever he made one of his involuntary, nasty references to her being the older, she brought him round, oddly shy, coaxing, to remembering that he had proposed to her before he asked her name. "Only of course you knew my name, you were just being fresh. I knew yours." And she always asked, "Did you really know you were going to marry me then; were you *sure*?" and he always answered yes because it made her glow and preen and he would not have known how to explain, or would not have trusted her to understand, that he had said that not because

he was sure he was going to marry her but because he wasn't
sure she could have meant to kiss him that way.

Hilary ran his hand down the bucket seat on Jadeen's side,
barely touching it. His ten minutes wasn't up but his im-
mobility was becoming unbearable to him. He flipped into
gear and pulled out to McPhay, thinking that maybe he would
run the length of the boulevard to Medical Centre and back in
hard full one-block leaps up to the lights. But there was a lot
of the dogged, dignified traffic that came in from the suburbs
for the evening, and by a freak somebody was pulling out just
in front of Cordoba Chambers, so he couldn't afford to give
up the space. He parked, went up the steps and showed his
pass—he did this in such a way that the expression "flashed
his press card" would describe it accurately—and although
for once he felt as surly as he tried to look, the same pride as
always surged up in him as he went on past the ticket man. He
was right about their starting late. It was eight-fifteen and
little Dr. Courcey was just getting up to make the introduction, the crowd still raggedy on the aisles and the place
humming. About a thousand probably. The lecture hall was
arena shaped with Dr. Courcey as the lady and Dr. Rugg as
the tiger—this made Hilary smile—and it flung the noise
around with echoes. Mrs. Courcey was bustling up and down
the back shushing university freshmen who didn't know
enough to resent it. Mrs. Courcey organized the evening series
and simply couldn't get over her significance; tonight she was
wearing a blouse that looked as if she'd had all the yellowing
family heirloom lace gathered up into one magnificent fichu.

To Hilary's angry surprise, the first person he recognized
after his father and the Courceys was Andrew Dodds. Hilary
had thought he was safe from that at least! There was an
empty seat in the row behind him and Hilary slipped into it,

saying, "Jesus, Dodds, I didn't expect to see you here tonight. Isn't I.P. interested in picket mobs any more?"

Dodds turned his great suffering saint's face ponderously around to him and said after a second, "Oh, it's all over but the boozing down there. I left a rookie on. Your daddy is too big a man to desert for half a dozen ornery stevedores, you must know that, Rugg."

Dr. Courcey blew into the mike, somebody turning up the volume till it dinned and dinged and stung your ears, and Dodds faced back around to the platform. Hilary realized that he should be pleased because it meant that in I.P.'s opinion he was covering the main event and Mendick had gone down on a rookie's beat. But of course he wasn't. He was irritated that he'd have to write the story tonight, mad that he had to cover Rugg's speech at all, and furious that Dodds had said "your daddy". Dodds had never said anything even faintly sarcastic to him before. It seemed to Hilary that his father managed to make himself directly or indirectly a party to every anguish and annoyance in his life. Dr. Courcey was going on about "the most revered citizen of our intellectual community," and down on the platform Rugg pulled in his chin, made surprised eyes and looked behind his chair. The audience chuckled approvingly, especially the freshmen. Rugg rose and shuffled up to the lectern, looking just as off-hand as possible in case anybody in the hall had got the idea he was a square. If he was given a joky introduction he always approached the podium pensive and austere. Hilary had stopped going to his speeches years ago and he'd forgotten how Rugg's effects were just about fifty per cent more obvious when he had the licence of a speechmaker. Now he remembered, and he also was reminded of the way that, when the *Centre Star* staff had come to their house to paste up a special edition for

April Fool, Rugg had spent the afternoon debunking journalism generally and high school journalism in particular, and the evening charming the holy asses off his staff.

Rugg announced that instead of detailing one operation or eye disease, tonight he was going to try "to give them a sense of the whole history, struggle and triumph of keratoplasty." Then he told a joke. Hilary didn't listen to it—he was watching the folds on Dodds's neck and marvelling that you can read a man's strength and sorrow even from the back—but he knew that a joke had been told because of the lecture-hall laughter that swilled around when it was over. Not the real enjoyment laughter of people running on a beach, but the hopeful, maybe-you-aren't-going-to-bore-us-after-all laughter that had made college seem so pitiful and silly to him. He could not imagine why one thousand people had gathered in this hall who were already reduced to gratitude that the speaker had told a joke they would not have tolerated in the Snack Bar. But then surely no one was quite as bored as he, and perhaps they had reasons for being here that seemed as pressing as his did. He tried for the sake of his report to listen for a time, but it was like trying to hear "mares eat oats and does eat oats" after you already know the song: no matter how you tried it came out "mairzy doats and doazy doats". After a while he took out his notebook and started doing some cartoon faces, a pendulous thing of Dodds that wasn't unlike, and one of Mrs. Courcey, nude except for the fichu. He tuned in just every so often to make sure that he'd know what to write: the vision of the great de Sevres, the paucity of Parisian corpses, Law and Medical Progress in an unwitting deadlock. Rugg said, "Luckily, you see, there was a war . . ." and the attention in the hall palpably intensified, focusing hard down on his at-ease, imposing face. Hilary focused on it too, saw the

121

steep features freeze for an instant as Rugg registered his success. Revulsion stabbed him and, relaxing his will suddenly, he let all the memories of his grudge invade his mind.

Using the father bit to flirt with her. Taking every opportunity to discredit him. Treating their engagement as the eighth dumbfounding wonder of the world. Scolding him for a dirty handkerchief. Surprising them that night on the porch. Taking Jadeen off into his den. "Oh, fahchrissake do call me Angus, I can't stand this Dr. Rugg business and if you start in with Father I'll feel ancient . . ." ". . . The most impressive quantity of babyshit you ever hope to see . . ." "Well, I don't know what you see in him, honey, but welcome to the ancestral manse . . ." "Oh, Hilary, don't look *embarrassed*, Jadeen's not a prude . . ." "Maeve, honey, hurry up and have that boy before this hot pair make him into an uncle, will you?" "Rotating supply! Rotating supply! Excuse me son but don't you think it's time to rotate this supply? Ha ha ha . . ."

Into the Reuzarne experiments, enjoying himself now, Rugg was wandering farther and farther from the mike, up and down on the podium, letting the back rows pitch forward and strain towards his voice. They actually did this, and Hilary raged. Dodds was scribbling away frantically in his notebook as if he were taking the whole thing down in shorthand, and once again, though this should have made him feel a little better, aloof and composed, it didn't. He wanted to shake Dodds by the shoulders for manifesting such absurd, energetic interest. What's wrong with me, thought Hilary, my God, My Problems Are Imaginary, it's not Jadeen, he flirts with everybody, he treats Mom the same way, and his secretary too, My Problems Are Imaginary. Jadeen, Jadeen.

"Hank Bordle's little brother Stuart," she'd said. "You remember Hank?" Hank Bordle who was penis-proud and

had stolen a ruler from the Registrar for the purpose of winning bets in the gym showers; whom nobody ever forgot
because he could unsnap a bra with one hand through three
layers of wool and silk and had once dared to do this to Ida
Bergen. But who had been in the class after Jadeen's and before
his so that he'd said, "Bordle? Vaguely." She'd dated Arnold
Pavageau, who'd been *Star* editor a full six years ahead of
him, and the other day he'd pretended to forget *his* name
altogether. This made him furious at himself but the fury
itself felt childish, it was a stone-kicking fencepost-banging
kind of fury. There would be more sense to it if Jadeen had
been in her nature older than he, or stronger willed or more
intelligent or subtler. But she wasn't and both of them knew
this, assumed it. All she had was a college degree that he
hadn't, an independent apartment that he hadn't, and a female
tenacity that he hadn't; and these things were of no moment
to anyone of any moment (not even his parents, who for all
their call-me-Angus and girls-together familiarity would have
hooted, *hooted* at the idea of this shame of his) so that it was
without any notion whatsoever of *who* could mock him as
Jadeen's junior that he feared so being mocked and so suspected everyone of mocking him that there was no one, no
one, no one he would have dared confess to. Except, one
afternoon he had had the oddest, most impracticable fancy, it
had come to him sideways on the smell of somebody's burned
pipe, that Millar Rourk would not have laughed.

A shifting of shapes in front of him brought Hilary back to
the hall with a start. Rugg was saying, ". . . Home from the
war, I found that others here had also been . . ." Dodds was
easing himself past flannelled knees to the side aisle, and when
he achieved it he climbed swiftly out of the hall without so
much as a glance in Hilary's direction. Hilary checked his

watch. Ten to, and since they started late it would run till a quarter after anyway. There was still all the business about perfecting the instruments and beginning with penicillin. Dodds had no particular issue deadline to make so he couldn't have been in a hurry, and it seemed odd for him to leave in the middle unless it was meant to be an insult, which Hilary couldn't see there would be any point to. If you were a theatre critic you could afford to leave after an act because that was just your opinion, but if you were doing a news story presumably you had to have some idea of the whole thing. Still, even if he was in the wrong, Dodds's going made Hilary feel gauche to be still sitting here. It was as if he were staying out of respect for his father, or even if not that, that he was too green at his job to risk missing part of the speech. Under cover of a few bored neck-stretches he looked for other newspapermen but found none. A.P. had only one night man and he'd surely be at the docks; apparently *The Chronicle* hadn't sent anybody, unless he'd already gone off too, in which case Hilary was left absurdly unlistening here alone, the only man who really knew all this stuff inside out and could have written his story without ever coming. Every once in a while the college and med students around him erupted into snorts or leaned over closer when Rugg strolled out of the mike range; oh, he knew how to hold an audience, all right, did old craggy-pored Gus Rugg.

Hilary fidgeted until five after, when Rugg started in on foundation grants to the present Centre, wanting to follow Dodds's example but apprehensive that his father would see him leave. When he realized that this was his principal reason for staying, he closed his notebook on the cartoon-covered page, nodded his excuses towards the aisle, and climbed out.

In the stairwell at the far end of the lobby Dodds was still

124

standing talking to, or rather listening to, Mrs. Courcey, whose squirrel hands were fussing hysterically through the lace business. Hilary went hesitantly in their direction, but as he neared them Dodds altered his stance an eighth of a turn, covering Mrs. Courcey and offering more of his back. Not sure it was intentional but not damn well going to give them a chance to make it clearer, Hilary breezed past them up to the bulletin board—Mrs. Courcey was saying, "Do appri*shi*ate the coverage . . ."—noted a few arbitrary dates from the school calendar, turned back past them and pushed out the centre double doors, feeling battered, feeling the hot fresh gusts of air that the doors sucked towards him, feeling glad that his car was no farther than the bottom of the steps.

Nine o'clock, Jadeen

Afraid of missing him, but unable to wait on the corner of Sampler and McPhay as they'd agreed, Jadeen walked on towards Cordoba Chambers, with quick attention to any red car, parked or moving. A few blocks away she relaxed a little because, although it was now nine o'clock, she could see that the lecture hadn't let out yet. The steps were still bare and the doors closed even when she got there, and Hilary's car was right in front: she peered in it to make certain and there sure enough was the bootie hanging off the mirror stem. That was Hilary, to find a space on McPhay at eight o'clock in the evening right in front of where he was going! It was locked but the vent window on her side wasn't latched and by twisting at an angle she could reach the handle inside. She got in and slumped as far down in the seat as possible, thinking wouldn't Hilary be surprised. But in a few minutes the position was cramped and felt like it wasn't doing any good to her already crumpled dress, so she sat up again and adjusted the mirror over to her side. She fished in her bag for a little jar of cream and tried to clean up the edges of her eyeliner. Her hands turned out to be a bit shaky though and she ended by taking the whole business off and starting all over again. She thought she would surely hear when the crowd let out, and have time to slide down out of sight for a surprise; but then all of a sudden Hilary was there opening his door, the first one out evidently, and he must have seen her from the steps. All the same he could have said something about

her being here: "Aren't you clever!" or at least, "Well!
Hello."

He just got in and sort of nodded to her as if he was expecting her and not any too excited about it either, automatically
reaching up to fix the mirror for the rear view although she
had her lipstick open, poised in mid air.

"Excuse *me*," she said, "but I wasn't quite done with
that!"

"Excuse *me*, but I have a story to get in."

"Well, excuse *me*." She sat back with the open lipstick still
in her hand, slapping her bare shoulders against the leather;
and then all of it, the slap especially, sounded so much like a
fractious middle-aged couple that she had to giggle. She saw
Hilary's hand hesitate on the starter with wanting to know
what the giggle was about; this hesitation made her love him
very much and she smashed her face into his sleeve.

"If we're going to quarrel, let's quarrel about what we've
got to quarrel about, O.K.? Because really I love you and I
can do my lipstick without a mirror."

He put his face into her hair, she felt his warm breath on
one ear while his hand traced the outline of the other.

"Really my story doesn't have to be in till midnight," he
said and then rubbed and pressed her shoulder and ended up
by slapping it, flippant, the way she had slapped the leather
with it, and this time it really was all right, or if not all right,
anyway better.

He pulled out into the now-sparse traffic and gunned the
half block to the light at a completely unreasonable speed,
skidding stopped so that she said in spite of herself, "Hi-lar-
ee!" and he turned and grinned at her. Then he got in behind
an empty flatbed truck and followed it docilely all the way to
the middle of downtown, tapping his fingers on the wheel not

127

impatiently but as if he were humming a tune in his head or counting something out.

"Bad time at your mother's?" he asked, and Jadeen, grateful that Hilary never invited crises or magnified molehills, although sometimes when she was angry at him for something little she found this exasperating, thought, well yes for heaven's sake I had a bad time at my mother's, that's all, it isn't the first and really it isn't the worst either.

"Pretty bad. I shouted and slammed the door and so forth."

"Good girl," Hilary said.

Jadeen noticed again how you could tell a fact and have it completely misrepresent the truth, such as saying "I shouted" which meant she shouted at her mother, which she hadn't. And then even though Hilary couldn't stand Mommy it was odd of him to say "good girl" because in this case he was really on the same side as Mommy, even though she wouldn't have dared in a million years put it that way to him and even though, again, it wasn't Mommy she'd screamed at but Miss Honeywell, whose side he was also on but she wouldn't have dared say that either.

He turned on to Alvarado Avenue and the tower of the newspaper building loomed up flashing ". . . condemned by Jerusalem court . . ." in lightbulbs before they were too far under it to see any more and Hilary swung into the parking lot. There was a sign on the bumper-fence that said "RUGG" in black hand-painted letters on a yellow ground. She hadn't expected this. She said, "My!" and Hilary punched her, jeering, but she could see he was pleased.

"Do you want to come up?" he said.

"Why not?"

He'd said that he didn't expect to have to write the story tonight, and both of them thought of it as an annoyance that

128

he had to after all, but now when the hum-and-clackety news-paper sounds started to reach them from upstairs she was excited to see his newsroom, and she could tell from the springy way that Hilary climbed the stairs that he was excited too.

She thought the room would be empty or have at most a half a dozen tired men sitting around telling cynical jokes in their shirtsleeves, so she was absolutely astounded when Hilary pushed open the double glass doors and she saw the huge hall jammed and bustling, the noise and the, something, *jumpiness* of everything reminding her of the cafeteria at Centre, people up and walking around a lot more—women too—than you think of when you think of a newspaper office.

"What is it like in the *day*?" she gasped. Hilary pretended to laugh at her, but it wasn't a laugh, really, it was just a catching for breath because he could see as well as she could what they were in for, although he was trying to hide it.

"In the day it's kind of dull. It's a morning newspaper, Jadeen, so of course all the news that's really news gets written between now and midnight."

"Oh, of course," she said. "When you're editor will I have to sit home evenings all alone then?"

"When I'm editor," he answered, "I'll build you a glass cage right in the newsroom and all the reporters will have to genuflect when they pass.

She giggled self-consciously. It wasn't hard to see where he got the glass cage idea from. The men began to sit back in their chairs and squint over their cigars as Hilary guided her through the desks up towards the front. Jadeen felt that her hips were swinging and when she tried to hold them rigid her knees went stiff too and her walk turned prancy.

"Well well well *well*," said one and somebody else said,

"Yas, Rugg, yas!" Jadeen told herself that they would do this to any female from a monkey upwards, it was part of the pose of being a reporter, it was nothing to get either big-headed or shame-face about. But she couldn't find the right expression, when she tried not to look too naïve and shy her chin came jutting forwards, sassy. Nearly everybody they passed at least gave Hilary a thumbs-up or a circle of thumb and forefinger, and most of them made noises as well. A woman reporter grinned at her in a way that said, you just have to stick it, honey. Hilary sailed on so exaggeratedly oblivious it was funny.

She was intensely proud of being with him, his girl, because he was a newspaper reporter and belonged here, but also because he was someone who could have a girl that other reporters would look up at and say, "Mmm!" That sounded silly when you thought it out, but it was so. It used to be different: when Arnold Pavageau had asked her out it tarnished his image and she was only partly glad, thinking without admitting that she was thinking it, well, he can't be much, I certainly thought he could do better than *me*! Now they were beside Hilary's desk and he pulled out a chair at the empty one next to it, gallant as no Hilary she had ever seen.

He sat down and for a half-hour or so wrote his story while Jadeen tried to read the first edition. She read the lead articles on the picket fight and the verdict in Jerusalem at least four times apiece, badly ashamed that she couldn't concentrate and felt eyes on her all around her, whether they were or not. She read them again, saying to herself, I really *am* interested in these things, and then saying to herself in desperation, they used fire hoses, they used fire hoses, six million Jews, six million Jews, six million Jews, but the back of her neck itched and in the end she gave up on herself and studied a picture of Princess Grace visiting a children's home with her hair done

130

up off-centre a new way. Once Hilary looked up and said, "Usually I'm quicker, but usually it's Bill Jorgenson sitting there, and he's not so distracting." She smiled at him and said nothing. It wasn't her that was distracting him, it was her effect on the other men, who kept wandering by keeping a really quite prim distance away from her but jostling into Hilary growling, "Yas, *hmm*."

But it was better sitting down anyway. She stuck her knees far under the desk and read the inside pages, making more of them. When she got to the sports she folded it up and toyed with a fraternity emblem in front of her—Chi Beta, one of the poorer ones at State, not even a national. She scorned fraternities and sororities altogether herself, but she was surprised and perplexed to see that whoever sat next to Hilary had belonged to such a bad one. Finally she felt secure enough to look around at the hurrying and scuttling, the men gnawing their cigars and tapping on their bellies as they thought something out, and a couple of them even wearing green eyeshades, just the way you expect in a newspaper office after all, once you got used to the busyness.

Finally Hilary got up and took his copy to the man in the hole of a semi-circular desk, and when he came back said they could go.

"I'd introduce you to Millar Rourk if he was here, but he goes off at eight. He's the best newspaper man in this town."

They did the gauntlet again the other way, but Jadeen was more at ease now and even smiled at the men Hilary acknowledged. She felt fine. All that at Mommy's wasn't forgotten, but it had got blended into an overall agitation not at all unpleasant, just right for a couple of hours' roasting jazz. I'm marinated for it, Jadeen thought.

In the car she waited for him to start but he didn't, he sat

131

with his right hand on his right knee and his left hand on his left knee, relaxed against the seat looking at the floorboard. Oh, it's going to be now, Jadeen thought, and the excitement turned back into fright and disappointment. She looked out at the "RUGG" sign and the bigger cars around them to place it, to fix in her mind the idea of "here" because this was not where she had imagined it. Oh, Hilary, she willed him, let it go now, let's have jazz now; leave it till walking in the quarter or at my place, where I'm at home.

She lay her left hand lightly on her thigh so that he could take it if he wanted to, but he didn't do that either.

"I don't like gestures, Jadeen," he said, quietly and finally.

For a silly minute, even though she really knew what he was talking about, she thought that he was talking about the scene upstairs, and she hoped she hadn't wiggled too much or anything on the way out. Mommy'd always said she was bold and she'd never been sure it wasn't so.

"Everyone says my father is a great man and I've never been able to see it because all I could see was his gesturing, his hands up in front of his face or a mediocre joke up in front of whatever it is he believes or feels."

It was odd, she knew that he felt that way about his father and yet she couldn't understand why it should be so. The very first time she met Angus she'd felt as if she'd known him for ages and could have said anything to him. Hilary was subtle and sensitive, if you did something to irritate him it took you a long time to understand how you were in the wrong; but Angus was so easy to know that it seemed fantastic his own son should find him otherwise. All you had to do with Angus was say, "What do you really believe, what do you really feel?" and he would tell you; if he thought you were genuinely interested he would work hard to tell you exactly,

132

huffing and puffing at it maybe but hiding nothing, saving nothing back the way Hilary did so that you had to pry at him and plead and examine yourself down to your smallest thought.

"Jadeen, if you do this, it will have the value of a gesture and nothing more. You'll say: Tantara, I'm for brotherhood; and you'll disappear into the north and in three weeks nobody here will remember you existed. There'll be a small scandal around your name, it'll shock a few people for a little while, and by the time people have got done shaking their heads over it, it won't be worth one slice of bread south of Whalley Avenue."

"That may be so, that's probably so," Jadeen said.

"It's so *easy* to do, don't you see, Jadeen. You make your gesture and then you're shut of it. You're morally and geographically out of the fracas. Anybody can do that. The difficult thing is to stay here and fight here, every day in all the plodding, irritating little ways, reasoning with fools and tolerating bigots. My God, Jadeen, supposing all the desegregationists in the south just pulled up stakes and travelled north. Wouldn't that help a lot?"

She felt her certainty and her reasons slipping from her like a pocketbook sliding off her knees. She always felt that way when she argued with Hilary. She felt stubborn and said, "Maybe I should teach in a Negro school."

"Oh, Jadeen, for God's sake stop playing Saint Joan with me. Have you got the physical courage to do that even if they'd let you?"

"No," she admitted sighing.

"Then why can't you recognize the thing you have got that's worth more than a whole regiment full of physical courage? You can *teach*, Jadeen, kids listen to you, mixed-up

133

explosive kids that don't listen to anybody. What difference does it make if you're officially teaching an official text that preaches black inferiority? All you have to do is avoid saying anything that will lose you your job. Jadeen, all you have to do is read some of the stupid sentences in that book very slowly and then smile and shake your head. All you have to do is tell them the way you told me: all albinos are geniuses and all geniuses are albinos. They'll get the idea, and they'll think about it all the more because they got the idea themselves, and all the more if they realize you don't dare say anything against it. You're clever enough to do that, aren't you?"

"Yes, I'm that clever," Jadeen said.

"Well, can't you see how much you can accomplish that way? All you can do in the north is tell the white north how wicked the white south is. Here you can sow doubts in the children of the wicked."

Something in that grated on Jadeen. Hilary's right, she thought, but for a split second she was tired of him and she had the sense that she was holding herself in, the same way she did with Mommy.

"Not quite fair, Hilary!" she said. "At least there'd be some other good, some publicity, people would ask me why I got fired and then they'd know in the north, and in the south they'd have to face it, that at least they *are* using a racist text in the schools. Or at least that somebody *thinks* they are."

"Gesture!" Hilary spat with real scorn, real contempt so that she would have thought it was hate if she hadn't known Hilary and known that it was disappointment. "Jadeen, are you really sure of your motives?" he asked harshly and Jadeen, surprised at how easy it was to say this, said, "No."

"I don't know, Hilary," she said. "I don't think as quickly as you do. I usually end up by understanding that you're

134

right, but it takes me a while and I don't like to make this kind of decision in a hurry. So far in my life I've only found two things really to love. I mean that: only two: you and teaching high school. If it hadn't been for you it would never have entered my head to love humanity, and for sure not justice. But you made me think about it, and now I've thought about it I don't see how I can go in and teach my students the opposite of what you've taught me and come out of it believing I've done my best for you and them. Don't be impatient with me, Hilary, I'm willing to be shown, I just haven't seen it yet."

He gestured and turned away from her. She knew that he was suffering and she was sorry, but she felt far from him as she almost always did when he was suffering, not quite knowing what it was that he was suffering from and having the callous, heretic impulse that whatever it was, she would not have suffered from it so. She thought how odd it was that she would have helped him convince her if she could, and she would have been so glad to have gone on to hear the jazz with it settled and done. It was like wanting the other person to win at tennis, but letting them win was worse than their not winning. He did take her hand finally and bent her fingers back until it hurt a little, letting them fall then one by one on the cap of his knee.

"You see, Jadeen, one thing that never goes out of my mind might never yet have entered yours. If I thought you were right in this, I'd give up anything to defend you, I'd follow you all the way up to the Pole if I had to. But I don't think you're right. I'd think you'd done the cheap and easy thing, and so if I went with you it would be *me* who'd given in on a principle because you wouldn't. I wouldn't be defending anything, I'd be giving in to you. I'd have let you run me north."

She heard all those conditionals, all those "would's"; she

135

was stunned by the clarity of them but she found that it was the clarity she was stunned by and not the idea itself. Since they first disagreed the idea of losing Hilary had been in her mind, even if she pushed it in a corner and set her back to it, even if she hadn't thought of how or why. She knew that a man's dominance was important to him and that you could spoil a marriage at the start if you tried to rule him. But that wasn't what she meant; she wasn't like that. All of a sudden something else that she hadn't thought about came to her, half came to her: a windy-grey idea of being, not with Hilary in a strange north and he showing where he lived and where he ate lunch when he was at university, but being *alone* in a strange north with the street signs not meaning anything and all her clothes too thin.

This picture hung for an instant in her mind, hazy, not the whole thing because there was also the alternative that Hilary would pose now, of her giving up teaching instead of him, for him; and she waited for it not knowing what to say and not knowing, even if she said yes, whether she would be able to mean it for year after year. A big house like Maeve's or an old one like Mommy's, thousands of little things to dust and you keep buying them so you'll have them to dust so you can feel in a hurry all the time, that there's work waiting for you. She wanted children but Maeve would have had two children and still have had fifteen years to dust, to atrophy until as she herself confessed she couldn't read a book any more. And Mommy sat on the sofa all day dressed for callers that didn't come, brooding about all the evil that could fall unbidden on a Christian soul. If she thought about Ida Bergen or Miss Trevelyan and said, "I wouldn't get like that," she felt it and knew what she meant by it, but if she thought of Mommy and said, "I wouldn't get like that," she was scared, she had no

136

picture of what it was she would be like instead. President of the P.T.A., Den Mother, A Pillar of Our Community, awful, awful; I want to teach.

Hilary still played with her fingers, letting them fall more lightly now. Ask me, she thought. I don't know what to answer but I'll feel better once I've said that I don't know what to answer. But although the question, alternative, was as plain between them as if they were saying it loudly over and over each to the other, still Hilary did not say it. Her fingers falling began to mark the seconds that he had not yet said it, still hadn't said it, *still* hadn't said it, until without her having noticed it go by the moment was gone when he still could have said it, and she realized with a rush that he had decided, that he was not going to.

Proving this, underlining it, he let go of her hand with a little toss, and in the second between his letting go and the hand's landing in her lap she thought, wait, Hilary, let it be clear to me, are you not going to ask because you don't want to compromise me either, or is it only that you don't dare, can't risk my saying no?

Then her hand landed with a soundless sting and at the same time Hilary flipped the ignition switch and said, spat, "Jazz!" and it was like that moment when the bell rings and no matter where you are in the middle of a problem with the logarithm still floating in the void outside your understanding, you put it away from you saying, "Later! I'll figure it out later!" and you award yourself now, for fifteen minutes or the lunch hour or the rest of today, whatever it is that your soul runs to without your having to lead it there. The car snapped backward out of the space and forward into the street, both of them quivering and the car too, and even though he turned forbidden left on the yellow light through the main intersection and other cars started hooting at them, the only word that Jadeen said was, smacking the seat side like a horse's rump, "Heeyoup-yah!"

The jazz was back in the old quarter in the storage half of a music store owned by Harvey Truax, the only landlord that Jadeen had ever known who really *looked* like a racketeer, hatchet-nosed and greasy blond, with a swaggery paunch although the rest of him was stringy. You came to it through a panache of other sounds beginning with the jinglebells of the hotdog cart on the corner, then a tiled bar where a New York City Negro tinkled away at Cole Porter and called it blues, then the sad run-down-carousel sound of two stripper joints in a row. There was a dignified old French restaurant and a couple of store-front houses, and then Son Alexander's drumbeats started coming up, felt through the pavement like runaway hoofbeats before they could be heard, and as soon as your ears found them then Kid Miles's cornet burst on them, crying to them: No! My poor Nellie Gray! while Albert Phillips's clarinet that had known it all along and learned to live with it by now moaned low, poor Nellie, poor Nellie, poor my sweet Nellie, and Ornery Lionel plumped at the bass pum, poor! pum, poor! knowing grief like a fat widow shaking her head but thinking of her own trials, not Nellie's, and Franklin Foster's boy banjo careful not to care at all, sitting by the river pulling at the collar of his mourning suit throwing stones in the water Nellie plink, Nellie plaw!

The entrance to the storeroom was a narrow carriage way, two doors in on the one side so that the only circulation was of the same stale slimy air. Truax's pale childwife stood shaking a coin basket at the gate, listlessly pleading, "Kitty contributions only, kitty only," and he himself stood beyond her in the forward of the two doors, leaning back to hear the coins above

138

the music but squinting ahead into the room at his stacks of untended records and his irreparable hung fiddles and his sweating septuagenarian band. His bare toes twitched in his sandals, his paunch made a great wet target with his belly button sucking at the bullseye, and he squinted blind in at the musicians, nodding time to some rhythm of his own that wasn't Nellie Gray. And all that stood between him and them was Daniel Collins, a stiff spindle-boned grad student from Seattle, who was their agent, who had come all this way to strike fire in them and make them play again, and whom they now forgave for having mismanaged them into a contract with Truax because there was a time when they, too, had believed you could do anything with love enough and only love.

"That's for the rent," Hilary said putting a dollar in the basket, "and that's for the men," putting in a nickel. But Truax only turned and smiled at him unperturbed and said, "Thy will be done."

It was packed, even on a Tuesday, with quarter artists and would-be-beats who came for the jazz or the idea of jazz, tourists who had heard about it and tourists who had just heard it, and a few like Hilary and Jadeen who had lived all their lives in this town and not known there was still this kind of music here until Daniel Collins came from Seattle and dug it out and delivered it in his innocence into the hands of Harvey Truax.

It was a bare room except for the records and instruments shoved and hung out of the way, with no platform and nothing to separate the musicians from the audience except that the musicians were black and faced the other way, opposing shined formal shoe toes to the sandalled feet on the front row on the floor. Jadeen and Hilary pushed through and made

139

space for themselves, Jadeen thrilling when Son Alexander leaned over his drum and nodded his sweet wide smile at them and gave them an extra radidiah! on the snare; Hilary waved at him sideways, Nellie plink, Nellie plaw!

Stocky Kid Miles, the leader and the youngest of the band at sixty-three, led them off loud next in "Mama Don't 'Low", and when the place was reeling and rocking brought it to a hard close, stern like the minister arriving, and took them into a blues so sick with sorrow you were ashamed to have been clapping. Daniel Collins said sadly over and over, "Yes, yes," while the men said, "Yas," and in the corner behind the piano a second-rate called Muskrat fingered the valves of his cornet and tried to look as if he were just resting and would join them any minute.

They broke for a while and Hilary and Jadeen went out for a beer with Daniel, listening through the list of grievances they heard each week against Harvey Truax, which expanded without changing and which Daniel went through now without passion, his anger sapped and his anguish inarticulate. When they went back Hilary put another dollar in the basket and said to Truax, "Buy yourself a pair of socks," but Truax, who was clever enough to have made a retort to this, knowing that Hilary knew he was clever enough, did not bother and said only, "Huy-yum."

The band wandered back in, Franklin Foster tweaking his catgut, frowning and shaking his head at it, always trying to pin something on his banjo, Ornery Lionel hopping and chattering in a Creole patois that only his bass put a stop to and that none of his fellow-musicians could understand, though they understood the bass all right. Son Alexander, biggest and gentlest-faced, sat down at his drums with the pleasure of a fresh cigar at the side of his mouth and began idly to fleck a finger-nail at the cymbals. He picked up a stick and let it fall easy on the tom-tom, smiling at the sound and adding the bass to it with his foot, having as his reason for playing the drums that he liked to hear them. His hands got more ambitious and his head cocked sideways always a little astonished at how the sound grew and grumbled and trembled and the cowbells struck in not so much a tune as an objection, the cymbals crashing in heavy on that from the side and the snare having a tantrum over it and then everybody speaking up together, furious, frenzied in Son Alexander's hands while his face with the cigar lazily smoking at the side of the mouth looked down on them, smiling with pleasure because Son Alexander liked to hear the drums. He let the quarrel fade out and end and then blinked when the applause came down on it, ducking his head for shy thanks and glancing sheepishly to Kid Miles, who forgave the unauthorized solo with an, "Mmm-*man*!"

They did "Yellow Gal" and "Maple Rag"; then a tourist was willing to pay five dollars to hear "The Saints", which they started in on weary and wry and ended with the same ringing rousing joy as if they'd just discovered it. Kid Miles, grinning and sweating and still having left-over energy to spare for the slapstick because he was only sixty-three, sent a few loud reports with it into the pause and said, "What would you like to hear, Mizz Jadeen?"

Jadeen said—she thought afterwards that it was perhaps because one of the beat artist girls that had made a point of staring at her stockings when she first sat down now turned up a face of frank envy, distracting her, making her feel smug and defiantly local—she said, "Oh, I'd like to hear 'Albert's Blues', please."

Hilary's hand stiffened in hers and she instantly realized

that she had done wrong, unforgivably wrong. Kid Miles smiled graciously and said, " 'Albert's Blues': a request number for Mizz Jadeen," and sat down, but of course he was wounded because there was no trumpet in "Albert's Blues" and she had returned the favour of the request by cutting him out of it altogether. She felt her face go red and all her damp crevices begin to prickle, her hair rising frizzly towards her scalp, and herself screamed at herself, oh why can't I keep anything right for half an hour? Why am I *always* wrong? Why can I never take pride in myself without being punished for it? Why can I never start to feel myself flow free without spoiling it with something clumsy? And why is anything clumsy you do so much clumsier if you do it to a Negro? Oh, I am so sick and tired of Negroes!

So she needed it more even than she had when Albert Phillips stood up and stroked his clarinet, lightly, deferentially, as if the song were in the clarinet and not in him and he wasn't sure he could coax it out. He was a small man, narrow-skulled like Hilary, not particularly dark but particularly luminous, with a network of thick blue veins on his temple that pulsed with his blowing when the notes went high. He was full as sick as seventy-five years of poverty could make him. The doctors had washed their hands of him, but he stayed dogged and dignified and alive because he willed himself to do it, and knew how. He kept his music haunted even when the others got hot. He hardly sweated and the creases held all evening long in his trousers and the sleeves of the shirts that he ironed himself. Nothing surprised his clarinet; he could hold all the grief he knew in the low register until he chose to let it out. He started there now on nothing but three mellow head-shaking notes, I'm so tired, I'm so tired, I feel so sick and tired; and then hearing himself say this, how sick he was and how tired came alive to him and he began weeping softly over it, saying in the slow lowering phrases, I don't want to weep, be weak, but I'm so tired, so tired. The bass said go ahead, go ahead, honey, go ahead, and the brush fell on the snare like sand scattered out of a shoe on the concrete square in the Larabys's vacant lot on the other side of the river.

Encouraged, the clarinet picked up its head and added: Lord, I wanted to ask you, wasn't there something else sometime? Don't I remember miracles in my mind? Lord, there was a time, let me remember, there was a time, wasn't there a time that I was let me remember wasn't I—*Free?*

The note sung and soared, hung startled at itself and wuthering overhead like a seabird off the bay that had come in once as far as the Larabys's vacant lot and hung, startled to see a girl dancing on a miracle, a cement square that they came and laid when they meant to build a store there and changed their minds. There were hot grasses like a blowing nest all around me and only one little bit of cotton to get in the way of the wind on my skin. And let me see, don't I remember, didn't they come back once and deliver another miracle out of a pickup truck, a piece of pipe you could walk through on your knees, and then didn't I have enough for a house and a stage, a ship and a train, a well and a tower and a cave and a cloud and wasn't I—*Glad?*

And didn't a seabird hang wuthering in the way of the wind on my skin, hot grasses blowing a nest all around me, and me dancing on a miracle out of a pickup truck and the sand scattered out of my shoe? And let me remember, don't I remember a miracle, that I was one with the bird and the grass and the wind and the sand scattered out of my shoe and wasn't I, Lord, don't I remember a miracle, Lord, that I was . . . good?

That was just about all of it now. The notes skimmed over it a few more times and lower with the memory fading, just to make sure, yes, that it was all there and that was all of it, bird, grass, wind, sand, shoe. Free, glad, good. Lord, it isn't that I don't believe in you. I always only believe a little less in you than I believe in me. So I wanted to ask you if there wasn't a time that I remembered miracles in my mind. Because, Lord, I don't want to weep, be weak, but I'm so tired. Seems like I feel so sick and tired. So tired.

At midnight they had to quit because they had no licence and after that hour the neighbours could complain, which the strip joints would because it looked bad to lose even two or three customers to half a dozen old black men. Hilary and Jadeen went into the littered courtyard and had a lukewarm beer with the musicians while Harvey and Daniel counted the money in the kitty basket. Jadeen always admired the way Hilary chatted so easily with the men and seemed not to talk about different things, or even to talk about them in a different way, than he did with everybody else. He could talk about integration with them, Africa, even the Black Moslems, and not look awkward the way she would have, although sometimes it seemed to her that the men were too old and were really not as interested in these things as Hilary. She herself didn't have to talk much but she made a point of sitting down by Kid Miles and asking him about his wife, recalling what a gumbo she could make—Kid Miles said yas that woman could make a gumbo, she knew her stew—and then asking him whether Nellie Gray was a woman or a horse. He didn't know either and they enjoyed themselves over that and she hoped it was all right about the request.

144

Finally the money was counted and Truax took his cut, called cheerily good night and headed upstairs, not able, though, not to turn around once and watch Daniel in the corner of the courtyard taking money, sixteen, seventeen dollars, out of his wallet to add to the money Truax had left him, to make up the union minimum for the band. Daniel paid the men and then, without even that businessman-face he used to use but that had never fooled anybody anyway, he marked down in his notebook the money he had paid out of his own pocket, drew a line, and subtracted it from the dwindling figure of his Seattle inheritance.

"Seeley's?" Hilary suggested then, and everybody said yes, yas, except for Albert Phillips, who dubiously asked Hilary, "Well, you going to take Mizz Jadeen on down there tonight?"

Hilary hesitated and Jadeen, suddenly scared, although she had to be up at seven, that the evening would be over already and she would be alone with Hilary again, or alone, said, "Oh, surely, Albert, just for a little while. It can't hurt."

"It's all over but the boozing down there," Hilary asserted. Albert bobbled his head to mean it was up to them, and Kid Miles clapped his ham hands as loud as, louder than the slapstick, and so they started off with another lift of spirits, leaving the courtyard past the rickety stairs where Truax's too-young wife was leaning over the rail, hanging back and looking wistfully after them on her way upstairs.

Hilary and Jadeen took Miles and Albert Phillips on scrunched up in the jump seat while the others piled the bass and drums into Daniel's big sedan. Seeley's was on the waterfront though it wasn't really a waterfront bar, it was too big and well lighted for that, too comfortable: married couples came here and sometimes wives alone together. Seeley himself was a big pompous high-yellow, who dared to let whites into

K   145 his bar maybe because he was so light himself, or maybe because on the waterfront the lines were blurred—after two weeks as a stevedore a white man looked creole and an Indian black and once in a while you even saw a black man pale from loading cornflour. Or Hilary's was the best explanation: that, the cops having their cut of his take, Seeley was not afraid of losing his licence, and there was no other form of police action that he minded much.

He came immediately from behind the bar to greet them, lugging his weight forward one side at a time and saying too loud, "Evening, evening. Always glad to welcome our white brethren to Seeley's," to which Hilary replied as pompously, "Thank you, thank you," and which embarrassed Albert so that when Seeley lumbered back to the bar he explained apologetically, "Well, Seeley, he's a kind of a bore."

They sat and ordered a pint of Old Grand-dad, which came with four jelly glasses and a bag of potato chips. There were more people than usual and it was a different crowd, though Jadeen couldn't have said exactly how different. Younger, maybe, swaggering a little and talking in a grudging, tight-lipped way without so much laughter. It made the air crackle. And the jukebox was louder, playing jazz, but a modern kind, nearly rock, which would make Albert go quiet after a while if it kept up, and would make Kid Miles with a few drinks in him start telling how the youngsters didn't care for nothing but their money no more, and not their music at all. Now, though, still in high form because it was only one a.m. and he was only sixty-three, he slapped his thigh and said, "Mmm, yas, man, we all know that kind of music: you hit me and I'll hit you, then you chase me and I'll chase you, then you run round the corner and when I catch up with you neither one of us will know where we're at. Yas!"

The others arrived, with Muskrat the second-rate, who had cadged a ride from them at the last moment and who was now repeating over and over to Daniel, "You just don't know the right people, man, you just don't know the real musicians."

Ornery Lionel, chattering to himself, immediately began to tightrope-walk a yellow line in the linoleum, which he had once been teased into doing when he was drunk, winning such accolades of laughter that he now never missed an opportunity to do it, drunk or sober. It was his Dumb Blonde act. It was funnier every time, so it looked like he'd never stop it. The place roared, strangers with those who knew the joke, and five or six white dockhands stopped in the open door, looked sullenly at Hilary, Daniel and Jadeen, and went on again.

They ordered another pint and it went like a swallow. Jadeen drank a lot, daring herself to keep up with the men, feeling even warmer than she had all day but not minding it so much. She went out back to the john and took off her stockings and put them in her bag. That felt good until she put her shoes back on and then her feet were damp and sore. She went back in barefoot with her shoes in her hand, waiting for Hilary to notice as she approached the table, ready to give him an I-don't-care look, but when he saw her he smiled wide and applauded without making any sound. This made her want to cry.

Son Alexander excused himself and said that, begging his pardon to Mizz Jadeen, he felt like he'd like to have a woman if they were all planning on staying there another half-hour or, well, yas, maybe forty-five minutes because he was getting on and seemed like he couldn't make it so quick any more. Everybody said go ahead, go ahead, and Jadeen giggled, which made Son Alexander blush. He left blushing.

The jukebox went frankly to rock and a few couples started dancing, which didn't ordinarily happen at Seeley's. There were a number of picket signs leaned against the wall saying, "Lever and Sloan Unfair to Dock Workers" or "On Strike Against Unfair Practices". A woman picked one up that just said, "Unfair", and danced with it, cheek to cheek and faintly dirty. This was a great success. Twisting in the middle was an odd couple, a tall chocolate-brown boy about nineteen and a buxom woman with straightened hair yellowing in streaks, not less than forty-five. The boy had no shirt on and his trousers were darker at the side seams as if they'd been wet recently, so Jadeen supposed he'd been fire-hosed. The woman wore a tight black skirt and a string-blouse that could barely contain her jouncing bosom, like two basketballs in a basket, Jadeen thought, even the colour. She looked at the boy's flat handsome sexy face, the nostrils flaring and the mouth ready to scorn, and she thought I guess it must be the bosom, I don't know what else it could be. The boy's muscles rolled, live animals underneath his flesh.

Hilary touched her knee with his and she turned round to smile at him, shocked at the abrupt pallor of his face, the narrowness of it, and the skin with no more depth to it than an eyelid or the skin of a newborn bird; his whole body linear and hard like something utterly foreign to a body. Troubled by this vision, she picked up his hand and kissed it, thinking, Oh, God! is it because I don't really love Hilary? Can I have made up the whole thing so I'll have to go away, get away from him, get out?

"D'you see that couple?" she asked him in a quick whisper. "That boy with the middle-age woman? Isn't that something?"

Pain threaded through his eyes and was gone before you

148

could be sure of it, but Jadeen remembered that she was older than he and was sure, thinking oh why can't I do *anything*, not *anything*? And, resenting that Hilary should add to her unhappiness instead of absorbing it, she emptied her glass and turned deliberately away again to the dancers.

"I'm telling you, man, you just don't know the right people," Muskrat said for the hundredth time.

The couple had finished dancing and the woman was sitting facing the bar, but the boy had his elbows on it and was propped pelvis-foremost on the barstool with his heels crossed on the floor. His bare brown chest made one shallow scoop from neck to navel, a triangular depression below his ribs the size of Jadeen's hand and glistening like rubbed wood, his fly swollen in general, on principle: he would have screwed the bar, night, September if he could. I wonder if his thing is black, Jadeen thought, surprised at herself that she should wonder this and then surprised that she had never wondered it before. His tongue is pink anyway but that's not the same because . . .

She realized that she was staring at him and that he was staring back, the blunt wet tongue was wandering on the scornful lip for her benefit, and now he was smiling at her just very slightly and sliding his hands into his pockets deep and slow. Her whole horrified instinct was to look away and hide, but her eyes did not follow the instinct, remained petrified on the half-open mouth with the full lower lip stuck just enough out to challenge and the pink tongue turning the corner lazy to run along the top. It reached for the scoop of flesh below the flaring nostrils and slid down again over the taste of chocolate. Jadeen felt vaguely that she wasn't breathing and intensely that her breasts were glowing, going hard, and she hunched her shoulders forward so her nipples wouldn't show through the thin dress.

"Ah-huh! Yeah-yas!"

The woman's voice was granular and shrill, the kind of Negress voice that can holler men in across a five-acre field or put cracks in a mud church wall when she gets God. Jadeen didn't know when she could have left the barstool but her body eclipsing the brown boy's mouth now loomed inches from her face, as awing as a close-up seen from the front row of a movie house. Her head appeared between, beyond, the string-bound breasts, no larger than they and the hair looking grotesquely like more string, the bright mouth raging and mocking.

"Yeah-yas!" she said again and all the noise died in the bar, leaving only the jukebox lurching and thumping stupidly in rock rhythm. Jadeen clutched the chair sides in blind panic thinking she's going to do something she's going to hit me she's going to kill me, but the woman, watching the panic with pride and hate, only moved her sweating body as close as she could to Jadeen's face without touching her, raising her chin so that she smiled mocking down from an even greater height.

"Mmm-*hm*!" she decided all at once and clapped her hands above her head. The clap rang like a shot and Jadeen's heart stopped: why doesn't someone rescue me? The woman clapped again above her head and, sinuously, cynically inno-cent, began moving sideward in time to the music, clapping until she was standing in front of Hilary. She began to dance for him.

"Mmm-hm, yeah, yas!" she chanted to the music, to Hilary, brushing his shoulder with her hip and then dipping away, running her fingers up her sides to lift and show the

150

bulbous breasts, not cups or cones like Jadeen's breasts but whole globes hung in flesh and revolving against each other now towards Hilary between the rolling forearms. "Hmmm, yas!"

She offered him the flat of her thigh stretched hard against the skirt, rocked and writhed in and away from him while Hilary smiled tight and polite and strained, sometimes clapping above her head until others began to do the clapping for her. "That's it!"

Franklin Foster called, "Seeley, man, could we have another pint here, and some other kind of music?" but the reprimand, cutting foolishly loud into the otherwise voiceless noise, failed of its object and all it brought was Seeley with a pint of whisky.

"Yas yas yas!" the woman cried, slipping the sleeves from her shoulders and addressing the quivering of her half-naked breasts to Hilary. At their table Muskrat began to clap with her and then, as Muskrat clapped behind and the woman clapped coaxing, taunting, in front of him, to Jadeen's incredulity and horror and despair Hilary too began to clap. "Yeah, yeah, yeah!" At the edge of Jadeen's awareness the chocolate boy clapped and laughed.

"Come and dance with me, white boy," the woman purred, her voice dropped down all at once to a sound like a thick river. "Come dance with me. Your lady friend won't mind."

The whole scene blurred before her, Jadeen did not so much see as feel the slow obedient rise of Hilary from his chair, and then, just before she ran, the swift breeze that was Albert Phillips brushing by, the grip of his bone fingers cutting into the flesh of the woman's wrist as he forced her away, "I'll dance with you, Cherita, honey. The white boy's tired tonight."

The two black figures moving a little off gave her breathing space, the breath she took of it burned. She ducked into it and for the second time that evening she ran away, barefoot out the open bar door and across the street, spurning Hilary's car and dashing a little way down the dock to clutch at the railing, thinking Hilary's right, I run away, I run away, all I can think to do is run away, turning her face to the river and weeping for the second time that night and wishing there were something to hide her face in, Mommy's hot honeysuckle. The river stank.

Two white stevedores stopped and called something down to her but she turned and screamed, "You go away, you just go, you go away!" so wildly that they did so, and then Hilary was coming out of the lighted doorway carrying her bag and her shoes and she screamed again at him, pounding her fists on the pier rail, "I hate you! I hate you! I hate you!"

He took her by the shoulders and shook her hard.

"What did you do to that woman?" he demanded and she screamed, "Nothing! Nothing!" knowing that this was a lie. "Nothing, I did nothing to her!" She broke away and ran to the other side of the dock, wheeling on him and shouting again, "I hate you! You'd rather see me humiliated! You want to! You're a nigger lover, nigger lover!"

He didn't come after her now and what she had said filled up the whole space of sky above the river and, astonishingly, for the first time in her life the phrase meant something to her so that even as she recoiled from it and wished she could take it back she thought, but he *wouldn't* have let a white bitch do that to me; and she understood something she had never understood before. But Hilary said raging and aghast, "Just what did you think I was?" so stunned by her simple vulgarity that there could have been no hope of her explaining that

152

there was another thing to be, something she could never be but had thought he was and had admired him for being: un-prejudiced, dis-interested, colour blind.

Albert Phillips came out of the doorway alone and Jadeen went to him and said, "Albert, will you take me home on the streetcar please? I'd like a gentleman to take me home."

Then something else happened, still something else, yet one more thing. She turned up towards the corner where the streetcar ran, assuming that Albert would be beside her and not knowing that he wasn't for three steps or so until, turning back, she saw him standing looking mournfully after her, embarrassed and sorrowful but rooted there to his spot with the blood pounding in his temple veins.

"Now, Mizz Jadeen," was all he said. She realized with shame that he did not want to take her home and would not; she realized that Hilary had seen it as well and, confused, she passed her hands in front of her eyes: I don't understand this either, this either. Are you afraid to be seen with me in the white neighbourhoods, or afraid of Hilary, or loyal to Hilary, or disgusted with me?

A terrible total tiredness flowed through her, she relaxed and let her head hang: never mind, I don't want to understand. Hilary took her arm and led her towards the car. Albert said he and Miles would find their way home all right, and thanks for the ride and he was sorry about any inconvenience to Mizz Jadeen and hoped she'd be all right.

She sat limp in the seat and Hilary drove slowly, saying nothing, except once at a red light when he laid his hand on hers and said without bitterness or blame, "You see, it just is complicated, Jadeen. It just is. All of it."

She let her head hang and her chin grate against the crumbled linen of her dress.

153

"Except whatever I do," she said dully. "Except whatever I do. Whatever I do will be simple, it will be this thing or the other. That's the trouble."

In front of her place he kissed her good night with a sadness yet greater than any she had ever felt in him; he said nothing about coming up. Her thigh knew his hand and began to tingle as it always did, on ordinary nights. Our bodies could make love now if we would let them, she thought. I wonder what it's like to be so much a part of your body, or your body so much a part of you, that making love will solve a quarrel, instead of having to resolve a quarrel before you can make love. We aren't very sexy, Hilary and I, she thought, and it was the first time she had thought this either. If I had a lover like the chocolate boy I'd be exhausted in a week and I'd be telling him he tried to make everything too simple. We suit each other, Hilary and I. We suit each other so much better than he has ever understood.

"I'll call you at lunch tomorrow, before I see her," Jadeen said.

"All right, my love."

She watched him drive away, she felt cold now in the early morning and went up. Her apartment was in a modern building where they'd pulled down part of the old Market, close enough to town to walk but far enough to have trees in front. She had a eucalyptus in her window, hung with moss. She had a wicker rocker that Mr. Terrance had given her out of the antique shop on Noon Street, a Queen Anne quilt from Mommy that she folded double on the bed-settee, all her books from school in a case that Hilary had made. She tried to fit these things into a trunk in her mind, the tree as well, but they poked out and bulged over and fell. There was no moss up north, or what they called moss was just a dense fuzz on things. She wondered how a eucalyptus would look without moss. Bare and bitty. They said snow looked like bomb rubble in a city on the second day. The moon was at half, hung blond in the eucalyptus veiled with mist and moss, her moon, her moss, her tree. Who am I to know what Right is, Jadeen thought, if everyone I've always followed tells me it's something else? I do wrong at every turn, how can I set myself up to know what Right is? If even *Angus* . . . And I'm so tired. So tired.

Four o'clock, Dodds

Andrew wandered in the parti-coloured light of Alvarado,
lights any colour but the colour of light, down towards Rouens
Street and down Rouens towards his apartment. The rooming
house itself was luminous from the marquee of the Orpheum
Theatre next door, a red gone visceral pink against the cracked
concrete. (Liddy used to call it the Perpheum Theatre and if
corrected would insist fiercely; he thought she thought of the
perfume of buttered popcorn.) It, the building, his home,
loomed amorphous in the night heat and in the city's fumes
and in his vision: not nude merely, but raw; painful anatomy-
pink riddled with darker nerves and pulsing slightly as the
neon perimeter of Ava Gardner's breasts next door flashed on
and off. Under Ava's breasts the smell of popcorn was over-
powering. The neon tube dipped up into her cleavage; her
open (laughing? singing? gasping?) mouth was the size of a
man's whole head; and there emanated from her and from the
building that fell away behind her bosom an all-engulfing
smell of popcorn: buttered, salted, sating, and more innocent
than milk. Andrew shed the paper from a saccharine drop and
looked up at the marquee, but the explosion of neon lacerated
his eyes. He could not afford this just now. He put the drop in
his mouth and stubbed his cigarette out on a marble pillar.
Real marble, too: the sight of them had made Liddy squirm
with excitement on Saturday mornings when, groggy, irritated at her gaiety, he had delivered her to the Kiddie Show.
The Perpheum Theatre. He didn't tell her he lived next to

the Perpheum now, although the temptation to exploit any tie was harrowing. She would beg to see it and he would give in; it would end badly for both of them, she shocked at his squalor and he shocked that he wished her to be, wanted her pity: she was twelve.

He had been wandering for he didn't know how long, hopping bars but not drinking, saying hello to dozens of faces he recognized but saying nothing else to them. The carbon of his copy was rolled up in his pocket, split and tattered, already old from his arm's brushing it all night. Now he wanted his shoes off and wanted this to the exclusion of any other thing soever. He had been watching the want grow until his thirst and tiredness and the need to urinate, all of which were more or less constant and so held only minor interest for him, had been usurped and totally ousted by it.

He was practised in pain, a connoisseur. He had known what it was that was coming—despair—by the surface of his skin, which went taut and vulnerable as a penny balloon. Any shirt would have been a hair shirt and casual touches flayed him. But being a connoisseur, he could do with less than this, and small distinctions fascinated him. The intensity of his feet's pain, internal and external, cramp and pinch and rub, was an unforeseen blessing into which he had let himself be gradually and totally absorbed. The wound that the little toe-nail had worn in the fourth toe on his left foot (the left had not been clipped so recently as the right) was in itself enough to occupy his mind and his entire being for several seconds. Here, under Ava, feeling for the key, he allowed himself the next and semifinal stage of absorption: to contemplate the enormity of taking the shoes actually *off*, letting his feet spread and settle on the throw rug like jellyfish in sand. This was troubling as well as delicious to anticipate, since once it had been done the obsession would pass as well. But he was home, was in the oozing corridor, on the hollow wooden treads of the first flight; and since it would have been dishonourable at this point to turn back, he thought about taking his shoes off as he climbed.

He climbed, let himself into his room and felt for the light. The room was a narrow rectangle with a vestibule converted to a kitchen, and shared its longest wall with the auditorium of the Orpheum. The movie played all night and this one had been on for several weeks: voices artificially resonant but inarticulate seeped into the room and he knew, instantly and unconsciously, where he had walked in on the movie that he hadn't seen. There were perhaps twenty different melodramas by now, the pattern of whose crises he knew without having understood a word of them. He learned the voices in his sleep, and when he remembered his past life the quarrels and recriminations returned to him in the same deadened-and-yet-exaggerated tones, their shrill intention inexorable although no single meaning could be grasped.

On his threshold Andrew flexed his feet in their cramped prisons and savoured the licks of fire in his arches and the balls of his feet. Delaying as much as could be considered legitimate, he hung his crumpled seersucker jacket on the folding-screen, opened his fly, relieved himself voluminously into the washbowl, deflected a jet of water around the bowl, and drank from his toothbrush glass. The water was tepid and tasted a little of rust. He pulled his tattered story out of the jacket pocket and rolled it inside out in his fists to flatten it, then filed it among others on the lower shelf of the oven. That was a shocking thing he'd heard tonight, but Andrew was not shocked. Not after what he'd seen of Angus Rugg this afternoon, and what he'd seen before under the skin of benevolence.

Squatting cost him dizzying effort at this hour of night and put explosive pressure on his feet, so he decided to abandon the delays and stumbled into the canvas chair by his bed. He hesitated once more. The floor was heavily littered with pyjama parts, empty cigarette packs and cans of Diet Drink; he thought of tidying it. But once in the chair his fatigue took hold of him; his flesh, that had been taut, became a ponderous, dragging weight. He couldn't face the effort of standing up again, and so at the last minute by default, and still eyeing the litter flirtatiously, he unlaced his shoes. He put a toe on a heel and slid one shoe from him; the stockinged toe dislodged the other—too late he remembered the rug and had to set them after all on the bare splintery boards. His feet distended, the liquids were allowed to flow in them again and as the pain passed out of them, which was itself piercingly painful, he prepared himself for transports of relief.

He was thwarted. Forgetting to pull the rug over had ruined it, and hesitating about the junk on the floor. *Coitus interruptus*, the withdrawal being as usual mental and of overwhelming insignificance: Frances poking him with her chin in the most arbitrary and infuriating way at just the moment that it would be too late to reassemble his concentration. And not just once, but invariably; her chin, her finger-nails, a sneeze. She had a talent for it. He could not forgive her for it, *could not*! and now his sticky stockinged feet on the bare boards were dully comfortable, six hours of walking wasted. She was always so sorry, so astonished, so tenderly submissive, faced with her clumsiness. Why was there nothing she had done that could not have been unintentional, when all his own cruelties were so blatant and so blameable?

Her picture rose out of the muddle on the window-sill in a gold dime-store frame, flattering her after the blurry manner

159

of female portraiture: her really rather drawn skin touched with an ethereal softness, her smooth bun and her wide eyes luminous, the eyes romantically earnest as well. Yet the picture caught—perhaps this was why he kept it—something about the rigidity of her mouth so perfectly that these studio fictions had all but ceased to exist for him. He knew that her expression in the picture was one of devotion and compassion; he now saw only the mouth, and, seeing it, saw with an intensity for which photography could have been no match whatever, an expression he had first noticed there ten years ago. Liddy, he remembered, had been doing something amusing. Stacking her books. Studying with two-year-old solemnity how to make a pyramid of them, while Andrew watched lazily, pleased with watching but not quite pleased with what seemed unnatural neatness in a child of her age. There was some imbalance in his insulin formula at the time. His last injection burned and itched, and he was scratching his forearm with deep, delicious strokes of his finger-nails. He noticed Frances in the door and was going to make some remark or other about Liddy's precocity, but the remark stuck in his throat at the expression on her face. The rigidity of her mouth affected the whole line of her chin and throat, as if she were making an effort not to gag. It was not a violent expression but this was of no importance because he recognized it as an absolutely genuine one. The moment passed and he seemed to forget it, but its genuineness turned out to have been unforgettable, a point of reference, a revelation only gradually revealed. Yet in a way it was no surprise: hadn't he always suspected that such excessive understanding was less like love than zeal? She was too drawn to beggars, too prone to buying orphans shoes. Too ready to exhaust herself in hospitals and Salvation Army refectories (such things show up so admirably in court) not sooner or later to show him he was her favourite charity. He couldn't remember what her mouth had looked like to him before. Nor was there anything in all the eventual violence that remained vivid to him; only that one original instant of betrayed disgust. He had lived with her for nine years of which five were the best he had known, and he was now incapable of conjuring any image of her face but that. By cold law, he paid more than half of what he earned in alimony because he had raised a temporary welt on her face. What did she pay, he wondered, and in what sphere of justice, for this permanent distortion of his vision?

Vision. Andrew shoved himself abruptly from his chair and drank another glass of tepid water. He was perspiring and shivering slightly in a chill produced of sleeplessness. He closed his eyes and steadied himself on the wash-stand, grasping at its grimy slipperiness and feeling his way along the edge to the flared spigot, the damp drain. His fingers touched the wall. He slid his hands along it. The texture conveyed nothing whatever, it could equally have been wood or paint or paper, and in a moment's panic he realized that he did not know the colour of his wall. He clenched his eyes against the temptation to open them and searched his memory frantically, running his useless fingers over the bland surface. Beige? Grey? Paper? Plain or speckled?

His floor was linoleum, he thought it was laid in sections. Yes, he bent down and could feel the cracks at about ten inches square. Encouraged by this, he remembered that it was green and white, the pattern laid at right angles to itself at every join. Andrew stood, feeling the depth of his fatigue and a certain foolishness; then stepped, hands before him, toward his screen and the night stand that should be just at its right. This was successful; the orientation of his last look carried him that far, but that was all. Beyond he began to fumble and miscalculate. The bed seemed impossibly far and the standing lamp several steps out of line. The texture of the lampshade reassured him again, the wound raffia felt so exactly as it looked as if it would feel, and it made a recognizably raffia-like crackle between his fingers. The old-fashioned fluted pole was less predictable, but he had never noticed it much, and the hard symmetrical ridges pleased his fingers: a discovery.

Hopeful, he resolved to discover his whole room this way, but he had stayed too long at the lamp and when he turned he had lost his sense of space and direction entirely. The lamp had been too far to the left so he must be back at the wash-stand; but he felt along distances of still-colourless wall and did not encounter it. His stockinged feet struck cans and cloth and he began involuntarily to mince, the fear of stubbing a toe out of all proportion to the pain it might have caused. It took a concentrated exertion of his will not to open his eyes, and this produced ridiculous contortions of his face, now tightly clenched, now stretched wide and his eyelids fluttering with the effort not to open. He was dimly aware of the changes of light as he turned or passed in a shadow, just as he was dimly aware of the rising crisis on the other side of the wall. Light and shadow seemed to glance off his forehead and he became afraid of hitting his head; he shied and ducked with almost every step. His own fear and hesitation inspired him with contempt. The humiliating absurdity of his posture! Surely he couldn't perpetually and forever move in dread of minor bruises!

What was that now? The side of a chair against the table that served for a desk. A jumble of objects, of which the least significant seemed most familiar. A bronze rhinoceros paper-weight, a coffee mug, empty, a clock noisily telling him noth-

162

ing. Other things more anonymous and meaningless to closed eyes: torn envelopes, bottles and boxes, ball-point pens. He identified a toast rack with the most frustrating difficulty, and then alarmingly identified not at all some leather folding object that could have been a passport case except that he owned no passport case. Something in cloth equally unlike anything he knew he owned, and then a wooden rod that didn't seem to be a pencil but didn't seem to be anything else either. Was it possible he had such paltry knowledge of his own possessions? He could begin to study them, but how long would it take to learn this room, and what hope was there of learning anything beyond it?

He reached his bookcase with relief and played his shaking hands over the spines, territory familiar even to his touch. He recognized certain of them and took deliberately down a battered favourite volume, his old college journalism text. He opened it eagerly and wiped the whole breadth of its glossy pages. It was cooler than anything in the sultry room; some trick of texture, the insulation of the other books, its position near the shaft. He rubbed page after page with the flat of his palm, talking comfort from its coolness; and then in growing despair he rubbed page after page as colourless as his wall, as unremembered, beginning to know the absolute blankness of unseen paper. He let the book fall and dropped to his knees, fumbling across to the oven and the thick collection of his own stories. The newsprint was cheap and brittle, more nearly ready to crumble than to yield him one sentence from its infinite blankness. He had knocked an empty can with his knee and it hit the wall, hit something, more than once, the sound reverberating unnaturally in his darkness. The sound mingled with the muffled movie and a new fear suddenly gripped him; an absurd, unshakeable terror that he was not

163

alone, that someone had entered, that someone was waiting in the hall, that someone was standing in the air shaft: worse: that no one was there but that once blind he would never be sure of it again, that he would never never know if he was alone. He sprang up and cracked his shin excruciatingly against the open oven door. He cried out with the pain and having cried out let himself go on crying out against the darkness. He opened his eyes. His wall was beige.

He lay on the bed and lit a cigarette with uncontrollably shaking hands. Frances looked across at him compassionate-eyed and brutal-mouthed. Dodds nursed his shin and the wound in his toe, his headache and the exhausted muscles over his eyes. He wondered what vision he would take with him into that final darkness; into what image a whole life-time's looking would finally condense, as his whole childhood condensed into the shape of commonplace and, for him, impossible candy; his whole marriage into the shape of Frances's mouth. He closed his eyes once more and waited for the image to form on his eyelids, recognizing it when it came: Angus Rugg, a false-hearty smile and patches of sweat on a rumpled suit; a pencil playing nervous drumstick on his taut, thick thigh.

Ten o'clock, Maeve

Angus was already at the hospital by the time she got up, but Hilary was still in bed and that made her feel relatively competent. Every month she slept later and got up groggier; when she thought about those six a.m. feedings she just put it out of her mind, time enough to worry about that once it was upon her.

In May when the real heat started Angus had insisted that she was to sleep through when he had early surgery. He'd see to his own breakfast, he said, and he certainly did! Maeve always came down to the kitchen with a little foretaste of amusement, disappointed when there were only egg smearings to clean up but carrying it with her all day as a pleasant joke to take out and shake her head over when there were liverwurst skins or chop bones. What this morning? Sardines! That seemed a little brutal to his patient, but then if somebody was far enough under the anaesthetic not to mind a blade in his eye, she guessed he wouldn't suffer from the surgeon's breath.

She cleaned up after him, wrinkling her nose over the sardine tin, then had an egg herself and forced the whole pint of milk down—better to get it over with first thing. She set breakfast up for Hilary, refolded the paper for him, and went out to the car. Angus left her the Packard to shop with on Wednesdays and went in a cab himself, explaining to her with figures and diagrams about once a month how, if he bought her a six-year-old coupé and they only had so and so many repairs on it and used so and so much gas, they would have paid for it in cab fares by such and such a date, to which Maeve always replied that for heaven's sake he didn't have to leave her the car, she could go and get the groceries in a cab! She might let him do it when she had the baby and Hilary was off married to Jadeen, but in the meantime it would have chilled her soul to see *three* cars sitting in the drive. They didn't even have garage enough for three in case it rained.

She slid gingerly under the wheel. *Much* worse than last week. Better go slow, if I had to stop sharp I'd give the poor tyke a whack across the shins. When I thought that last week I thought thighs; I wonder if she's dropped. I'd really better go in a cab next time.

But there wasn't much traffic and by the time she'd gone ten blocks she was out of the range of her afternoon walks so that it was a pleasure to go slow and see the not-quite-so-familiar sights. A new set of stores staked out on Jericho Street, the apartment on Whipple six stories up already, building, building. Swaggerman's itself was, she noticed as she pulled into the lot, clearing off the space next to the drugstore to add yet another wing. Whatever could it be this time? Indonesian and Andalusian specialties. Whalemeat lockers. The Saki Shop. Swaggerman's had been here for ten years and Maeve had been coming Wednesday mornings all that time but she had never got used to the profusion and its range. Sometimes she even—not always, but pretty often for a forty-year-old woman, when you thought about it—hesitated before the swinging glass door and closed her eyes under pretence of looking for something in her bag, conjuring up Cairny's Victuallers with its dirty stucco and the cowbell on the door, repeating over to herself: a quarter pound of bacon, two cabbages, a stoneweight of spuds and a half-ounce Mc-

Kay's Cut Plug. Then she opened her eyes and walked quickly into the midst of the citrus that was first on the right, California oranges and Arizona oranges and Florida lemons and Spanish lemons and African grapefruit and Israeli tangerines, piled in careless glorious pyramids like gold pieces spilled from a hand. And that was nothing. You could spurn those, scorn those for slippery shining apples and peaches the colour of slapped skin, grapes in tumbling pale and purple masses, pears, bananas, berries, honeydews, apricots and nectarines all with bins below at the level of your knees where, if you didn't mind a spot or a split skin now and again you could have them practically for nothing. And then dipping deeper into the lighted length of the store and getting ever more exotic, pineapples and coconuts, mangoes, avocados, figs, plantains, breadfruit, passion fruit and pomegranates. Then with the pomegranates it ended and you were hard up against reality at the spuds again, except not here, not at Swaggerman's, where potatoes were just the beginning of the vegetables that ran the same route down to salsify and wild orange mushrooms at the other end.

Maeve rolled her silver double-decker cart along and filled it slowly, thinking the week's menus out and doubling back when she changed her mind. She dawdled over the meats, wanting something special for Angus today that would make him look up and perk up, he'd seemed so tired when he got home last night. Too early for game, too bad, pheasant would have been just the thing. She'd have to choose soon because her back was starting to ache and she still had all the packaged and dairy things to do. Such distances there seemed to cover here: Maeve thought that all you had to do to bear a child of tired loins was to do your shopping in Swaggerman's eight months along.

167

She decided to try the tended counter and there in a bed of fresh parsley with a wee crabapple stuck in its tiny-toothed mouth was a suckling pig, pink legs stiff and tail curled and a sweet smug look to its snoot. Well, wouldn't Angus just love that! Expensive of course but she'd taken spotted pears and just for once . . .

The foetus gave a lurch and thumped at her, a rolling tickling kick through water, and slowly but continuously and then violently her womb contracted. Maeve thought, oh, sweet Dareena, love, hang on a bit, not here in Swaggerman's if you please; but the contraction passed without going into pain and she knew it was a false one. The foetus thumped again, lord help me a hard right to the bladder, all right, we won't have suckling pig for heaven's sake. She laughed at herself for this and told herself that the Irish were superstitious fools, but when the man came she ordered sweetbreads and took the package off pushing the cart before her at a good clip, hoping she could make it to the ladies' in time. What ninny would drink a whole pint of milk?

She turned down the rice and redbeans aisle and saw Dodi Samson coming towards her about ten yards away. Dodi's cart swerved when their eyes met and veered half around a corner before she stopped, visibly deciding that it was too late to duck off. Dodi, dear, thought Maeve, don't do anything dutiful now, I'm sure you're in a great rush. But Dodi was already huffing and waving her way, calling, "Why, Mive Rugg, isn't it a pleasure to see *you*, though! This morning!"

Dodi Samson was short and ample, about five years younger than Maeve and trying hard to stall. She was bra'd and corseted into a trim little bosom and bottom, which unfortunately left some spare flesh over at the armpit, midriff and thigh. Her husband Chick Samson was a third of the anthro-

pology department at the University, and Angus had been
intrigued by his ideas for a while, more gewgaws. They'd
tried to make a social thing of it but it never worked out:
Chick would be explaining the menstrual ritual of the Cana-
dian Tlingit and Dodi would be crying, "But you can't mean
it! You've *never* shaved your *legs*!"

"Hello, Dodi, such a long time," Maeve murmured, set her
weight on one leg and clamped with the other. I could just ask
her to watch my cart, but then we'd be committed to have
lunch together, sort of, and I wanted to get the crib assembled.
Maybe if I don't encourage her she'll run herself out in a
minute.

"Why, Mive, you look simply marvellous, marvellous. Of
all people that I never expected to see in Swaggerman's today!
But you're just amazing. I mean . . ."

She paused with the queerest furtiveness and Maeve wondered, a little annoyed, just what she did mean. Presumably
there was nothing particularly olde-worlde about going to the
supermarket when you were pregnant. On the contrary, Dodi
boasted to have been ski-ing in Vermont when her second
came, which Maeve thought was probably a lie, and a
vulgar one at that. Dodi cast her eyes about and settled them
on the crest of Maeve's pink linen protrusion, inside which
the foetus was getting restless and direly threatening her control. Dodi cleared her throat, either unable to take her eyes
away or else unwilling to meet Maeve's. Of all the absurd
insulting idiocies! It's as if I were sixty-five! What am I to
do, go into confinement?

"Well, and how *are* you?" Dodi asked.

"Wonderfully well, thanks. You and Chick?"

"Fine, just fine. And, ah, Angus?"

"Oh, overworked as usual. He's fine."

"Well, yes. He's just amazing isn't he. You know I said that to Chick, Angus is one of those men, he goes right along and nothing stops him, nothing at all. Well."

Just brilliant, Maeve thought as Dodi's eyes made a desperate tour of her belly. If the sight of me makes you so uncomfortable as that, why *don't* you take yourself *off*?

"And then anyway," Dodi went on with an unstoppered sort of rush, "one reads such dreadful things in the paper you don't know what to believe. I don't mean *believe*, I just mean that really life is getting so complicated isn't it that one doesn't know *where* you are, anyway like the old days. Chick says that, everything is so com-*plex*, really it's a pleasure for him to get back to his Indians though I tell him he ought to be more grateful for our advantages and the one thing comes with the other, doesn't it?"

"Yes, it does," said Maeve, amazed.

"Well, I won't keep you because I'm sure you'll want to get on home to him. I expect you're about due aren't you, Mive, that's marvellous, marvellous, but you mustn't let yourself get upset, that's all that counts. For the Baby. Well, I don't mean any of that business about playing the piano or going to museums, that's just old wives' tales, but the *nervous* system really does. Chick says scientists believe it ever since Freud. So chin up, huh? Your *friends* are with you, honey."

She gave Maeve's arm a squeeze and puckered her face encouragingly and went swiftly along, leaving Maeve staring blankly for an instant into the bug-eyes of an Italian chef in a spaghetti poster. Well really, just really! I wonder if I ought to order my coffin brought to the labour room. Of all the silly little chits.

Exasperated and delighted both—something to tell Angus —she sped on to the ladies' room and relieved herself, a piddling little trickle to cause so much agony, and then went on with the rest of her shopping, an eye out for Dodi all the while to avoid her.

She saw the bags packed, paid, and then directed the boy out to the car, remembering at the last minute that Angus would want a morning paper from the capital to check whether the wire service carried his speech.

She went back to the drugstore and picked one off the rack, scanning the lower folded half to see if it might be on the front page. It wasn't, but then it was usually inside unless things were pretty dull. She turned it back up to glance at the headline, a dense double banner this morning. A band like the sweatband of a too-tight hat constricted around her forehead and sent weakness, water, down through her veins.

Angus. Angus.

Eleven o'clock, Hilary

The aquarium was built along a narrow tunnel so that each window of lighted water and luminous fishes stood out in sharp relief. At the far end came an old man dressed like an English town crier in a striped muffler and a visor cap, carrying a lantern without a light in it. In fact it was not a lantern at all, it was a bell. Every time he swung it forward and up it began a shrill monotonous ringing that continued until it reached the apex of the arc and started down again. This was the warning that the aquarium was closing. Hilary could see the old man clearly, and could see the bright tanks across the tunnel from him, and could see his reflection in the glass of his own tank, though this was somewhat more obscure than the others because of the undulations as he treaded water. He was naked except for a pair of green rubber fins that made him feel gangly and did not help him to swim but kept him from getting his feet to the bottom. He began to worry because he wasn't sure that anyone knew he was here by mistake and he didn't know how to tell them. Also, he was supposed to be tropical and the water was too hot. It made him sweat. The sweat was oil and would not wash away.

Jadeen came along and read the inscription on his plaque. He couldn't read it even when he pressed his nose against the glass, but he felt certain that it was inaccurate, and this increased his discomfort. Jadeen stared at him without much interest; she seemed sad and took off her shoes. He saw her do this well enough to be sure that it was this and nothing else

172

that she was doing, yet he did not see it steadily; there seemed to be blank spaces in his seeing of it. Thwarted, he looked again at his reflection and realized that hair had begun to grow out of his mouth, waving gently upward in the water in front of his eyes. He was intensely ashamed and wanted to tell Jadeen that this was part of their mistake, though he didn't think it was and Jadeen, in the now narrow and fluttery glimpses he had of her, did not seem to notice it. She was reading the plaque again and crying softly and Albert Phillips had her hand between his two hands, patting it in soft re-assuring claps as with a slapstick, the heels together. The crier came past and Albert led Jadeen gently along with him, the bell gave one last shrill ring and they all passed through a metal door that slid from both sides and shut in the centre.

The telephone didn't wake him but he got used to its rhythm in his sleep so that its stopping did. He woke sudden and sickish, with the feeling of afternoon so strong on him that at first he didn't believe his clock and stumbled out of bed to check his watch. He was due now, but if he raced he could make it only a half-hour late. The idea of this rush discouraged him so that he sat for a minute on the edge of the bed, staring with distaste at his long toes and wishing he had slept through altogether. The grey and maroon stripes of his pyjamas seemed particularly unbearable, running moronishly lengthwise on all his limbs and crimped behind his knees. Disgusting pyjama colour. He could tell them he was sick.

But Jadeen would call the office at noon, and unless they happened to say he was home she would think he was out on a beat. He dressed hurriedly and ran downstairs, bolting a cup of cold coffee while he spread the paper out over the sink and checked his copy. The story on the speech was tucked on the

173

inside bottom of the third page, and had no by-line, but it was word-for-word, which was something because Link, the night editor, was a hair-splitter and generally hostile to day men. In the margin Rugg had scribbled, "Sounds like a dull dog all right." The telephone began to ring again, ear-splitting shrill. Hilary left the paper on the sink and ran out, his body set so sluggish against it that he seemed to be slogging through mud. All the way downtown Jadeen stood in the curve of the windshield, barefoot, pounding her fists on the dock rail and screaming at him. He looked deliberately right and guided himself by the curb, but she stayed in the corner of his eye. I haven't time, I won't think. There's the airline office opening, and bids on the civic theatre will be announced. Sure to be something to cover for freshman week. I came out of it badly but she came out worse, and she knew it. She'd look foolish now and if she looked foolish she'd have lost half her reason for doing it, she wouldn't do it for spite. Something will be damaged between us but I can repair it, all I need is patience and will and my wits about me, the same as I've always needed.

With a little luck he wouldn't have been particularly missed, and if he came in looking busy enough it might just be assumed he'd already been out on something. Rourk didn't much care when people arrived, for that matter, as long as the copy was in on time, and Hilary had a good record for that. Probably nothing would be said.

So he was taken unawares and astonished when he sprinted up the steps and saw, before he had even pushed through the doors, Rourk prowling this end of the room and making for him as soon as he reached the landing.

"Umph," Rourk said and wheeled, beckoning with a low, stiff-handed jerk. His face was bloodless and set, the back of

174

his neck looked blue. Frightened, Hilary felt or imagined a tension in the men he passed, made up of phony concentration and sudden silences. He had never been more than five minutes late before and it didn't seem credible that anyone could take it seriously. It must be something else. His head began to ache, or rather he realized that his head had been aching ever since he got up. He wondered if he had any aspirin in his desk and what he could possibly have done wrong enough to turn Millar Rourk's red neck pale and make him head—where was he heading?—straight back past the city desk towards the linotypes or the press or the john.

The john. There was a minuiscule lounge, large enough only for two ugly overstuffed chairs and a table where the men who came with lunch bags from home always ate. The table had a pile of newspapers on it and the neat peelings of one apple, curled up on a piece of waxed paper and turning brown. Rourk said, "Alone here," in a voice hard and something else; humiliated, maybe because when he admitted the need for privacy he had to admit that this was the only place he could get it, in the toilet with the browning apple peels. He indicated a chair with so awkwardly formal a gesture that Hilary felt an obscure, immediate necessity to refuse. The words, "Thanks, I prefer to stand," mounted to his mouth as if he had rehearsed them for a play. He didn't say them, but he didn't sit either, and this struck him as so funny that his body jerked and a ragged snicker came out. I'm a little hysterical, he thought with surprise. Rourk looked sharp at him and his mouth turned hard.

"Have you seen your story on the med lecture last night?"

"Yes," said Hilary, mystified, racing over the look of the story in his mind, seeing not the words but the slugs of type on the page, searching for mistakes as you search for them in a piece of knitting, as if you could poke your finger through the flaw.

"Have you read it?"

"Yes."

"Read it again."

Rourk flipped the top copy of the *Morning Watch* on to the table from the pile of papers and opened it to Hilary's story. Hilary sat then and read it with fitful concentration, looking for his sin. A misplaced comma here? He'd used "which" for "that" one place. Should "trustee" have been capitalized according to the style book? But that was the copy desk's job, and otherwise . . .? It was well organized, clear and complete, especially considering that Jadeen had been sitting at Jorgenson's desk and nearly every member of the night staff had contrived to poke him in the shoulder blades while he was writing it. If Rourk had sent him one of his manilla scraps with "Good story" on it, he wouldn't have been particularly astonished.

"Well?" he said looking up. He set his mouth as hard as Millar Rourk's, to show that he was giving no ground. Rourk searched his face for a minute and Hilary, more and more frightened, turned also angry, thinking, all right, I'm impressed, now what have I done?

Without shifting his focus Rourk reached sideways and took the next paper off the stack, opening it on top of the *Watch*. It was the first edition of today's *Chronicle*, still wet from the press. The photo of his father was so familiar that it took a few seconds to be shocked by seeing it. It was a profile, smiling, that Maeve had taken at Lake Charlebeau one day a few years ago and that Rugg gave out to anybody who asked for a photo because there was wind in his hair and it made him look outdoorsy, which he had always liked to think of

176

himself as being but never had been. The *Chronicle* had published it half a dozen times before. But not on the front page and not . . .

SURGEON CHARGES ALLIES USED
GERMAN POWS AS GUINEA PIGS

Hilary stared at the headline incredulous and ready to laugh. I'm still in the dream, he thought, but the instant he thought this it rang wrong. Whatever else a dream is, it is luminous, it offers something terrible or precious just below its surface. Whereas this had the heavy-handed logic of a human practical joke, something the boys worked out over coffee, everybody chortling. He tried to remember the date to see if it was April Fool's, but the date had gone out of his head entirely, he couldn't remember the month. He glanced at Rourk. The hard waiting expression hadn't altered and with a sudden electric jolt Hilary understood that it was meant, was serious, that they were going to distribute, deliver, *sell* newspapers with this absurd headline on them and his father's smiling profile rising out of a soft-collared sport shirt that he'd been wearing over threadbare swim trunks at Lake Charlebeau, but you couldn't see the swim trunks. He looked at it again and his eyes leapt down the subheads in the two-column story, "Auschwitz Among the Allies?", "Prisoners Blinded in Experiments", "Claims Military Still Has Files", "Security Breach Involved?", "Students Staggered and Dubious". The name of Courcey jumped at him and he read that Mrs. L. S. Courcey, wife of the university trustee and director of the Medical School evening lecture series, had expressed concern for Dr. Rugg's health and said that she had before seen evidence of his being under severe mental strain. Rugg was known among students and colleagues as a popularizer, she added, but the lecture was "his most unfeeling".

M   177

Beside this in a "Special" box was a short straight-faced item noting that the *Morning Watch*, local newspaper on which the son of the eye surgeon was employed, had carried routine coverage of the speech that had shaken the nation and the world. Dumbfounded, Hilary looked at Rourk once more and this time Rourk dropped his eyes, dropped himself into the chair opposite and began monotonously turning over the rest of the papers in the stack. *Baton Rouge Morning Star*, Special to the *Star* by Andrew Dodds; *Chatanooga Despatch*, EYE DOCTOR DIVULGES WAR SECRETS; *St. Louis Times and Post*, Special by Andrew Dodds; *Chicago Chronicle*, METROPOLIS ROCKED BY SURGEON'S ALLEGA-TIONS; *New York News*, by I.P. correspondent Andrew Dodds; Hartford, by Andrew Dodds; Montreal, by Andrew Dodds, mounting up toward the Pole until the stack ran out and Rourk pulled a coil of long wire service despatches out of his pocket and unrolled the reactions down the other side of the globe, Britain horrified, Moscow admonitory, Bonn knew it all along, Paris denies it, Jerusalem stunned.

When this stack lay curling on the table like the apple peel they sat both of them silent over it for a while, then Rourk got up and prowled the little lounge like a panther in a packing-crate. Hilary sat with his eyes on the caps of his knees under his cotton slacks, feeling the two sides of this imbecility, the home side and the *Watch* side, like two heavy gears that wouldn't mesh; but thinking of nothing, not even his father, not even Jadeen.

"Sasson wants you out of the office by noon," Rourk said at last, stopping. Hilary nodded dumbly and Rourk came closer, his dark eyes peering sharp and dissatisfied, as if there were something else Hilary could have done or ought to have done.

"He wants me out by the first of October," Rourk said.

178

Imbecility upon imbecility. Hilary put his head in his hands and tried to think of something that would serve as a reply to this, but all the space of his brain was filled with one in-articulate protest, rage in laughter. He heard Rourk pacing again and his arms thrashing into the chairs and the dis-patches.

"According to Sasson, you see, you were trying to protect your father, and according to Sasson I'm an incompetent for sending you to cover it."

"Jesus, Rourk!" Hilary burst out then. "This is a joke, it's a poor weak fucking joke! Anybody who's been to dinner at our house has heard this stuff, it was de-classified in 1950, my dad's written sixty monographs on it, it's been published in every medical journal in the country. Rourk, this is Dodds out trying to make an extra buck, you must see that. This isn't *news*!"

A look of pure hatred spread over Rourk's face and he rolled the dispatches back up and folded the papers deli-berately one by one, each with a slap like an ironic exclama-tion mark to Hilary's sentence.

"What *news* is," he said, "is what a *news*paper reporter has got to know, Rugg. I don't blame you for not writing this story. But if I live to bury you I'll never forgive you for not seeing it."

The hate went out of his face and the humiliation came back, his mouth twitched and he lost his force, he was a homely middle-aged man who'd just been chucked out of a good job for incompetence through the fault of his favourite rookie. Hilary felt himself engulfed in shame and regret and love.

"There's nothing I can do?" he asked, anguished, making it a question even though he knew that there was not and he more than half meant it as a cry of disavowal, withdrawal, as an end.

"Of course there's something you can do," Rourk said heavily, and sat again. "What we need to save face is an exclusive. Not a quote from an old friend that we can stick an 'Exclusive' on top of, I mean a real exclusive. Something *no* other paper can get. What he had for breakfast and what he says to his wife and how he reacts to the press before he figures out how to act in public. We need an inside story, a really inside story that everyone else will have to copy and paraphrase and rearrange because nobody else can match it no matter how much research they do."

"Rourk," Hilary said, "it's my father." They sat silent again for a longer time with the hum and rattle of the city room coming steadily and muffled through the wall, and for an instant of this time it seemed to Hilary that the worst of the whole idiocy was that he should be forced to say those particular words in refusal to Millar Rourk, should have to sacrifice Rourk to his father in a pose of loyalty, mocking farrago of what he most felt.

Rourk stirred heavily and gave a painful, unconvincing laugh. "Well, it's a bitch of a business," he said. "You've got to cut and pry to do it right, much the same as a surgeon, you have to steel yourself against certain ordinary kinds of feeling. If you really succeed I guess you come out of it less than whole. Do you remember when Coach Hurley turned out to be giving some extra-curricular workouts in the locker room? Story broke on a Saturday morning, we'd gone to press and the *Chronicle* would have Saturday night and Sunday on us before we could come out with a story. For those two days I was in such agony I couldn't eat or sleep or sit down, Rugg, and do you know that until we got our issue out on it Monday morning it never registered with me that there were individual human beings involved. A bitch, huh? And yet you know the healthiest thing about this country is that they let us poke and pry and disembowel sometimes, if that's what's needed. But with the blame, always with the blame. A surgeon slices into you and doesn't much care if it hurts, hopes it does; and nobody much cares that he doesn't care as long as they trust him to have the health of the whole body at heart. But us: if we weren't so nosey and nasty the politicians would have pulled the whole skin over the people's eyes by now, but nobody thinks of that. They say: Hooray for the Freedom of the Press, ain't the press fucking filthy, though!"

"No, Rourk," Hilary said.

"And in a case like this for instance we might really be able to do some good, give the other side for once, because they're going to rake your dad over the coals one way or another, Rugg; make no mistake about that. Either it's true and he's betrayed the human race or it isn't and he's betrayed his country, and by the time they get done with him, just you watch, they'll have him a liar and a Nazi both. And the only hope he might have for public opinion is if somebody took the trouble to make him look human in the press, holes in his socks and he's exhausted and his wife brings him a cup of coffee. Then at least somebody might say, poor devil, he made a bad mistake."

"No, Rourk," Hilary said. He rose trembling. "I guess I'd better clean my desk if I'm going to be out by noon. I'm sorry, Rourk. Good-bye."

"Great! Just great!" Rourk's voice rasped and raged behind him as he opened the door. "Clean mine out as well!"

Hilary headed into the newsroom towards his desk, but there were eyes on him and the noise pounded in his head. He wasn't sure he would make it and he veered left again towards the outside, thinking, I can come back and get my things later, there's no reason I can't come back later just to pick up my things.

Noon, Rugg

Rugg bought *The Chronicle* at the hospital stand and skimmed it descending the white stone steps towards the taxi rank. He knew the steps and did not need to look at them. He let spring two fingers from his thumb in irritation at the story, the same gesture that he used to kill moths on the screen porch screen; and he told himself that newspapers were a bloody damn nuisance and he'd always said so. He rolled the sheet into a loose spiral and threw it into the taxi before him. He was angry, but to be angry cost him no effort and did not engage his mind.

He was still seeing that eye under the trepan, an amber eye with a remarkable burst of orange flecks around the pupil, tapering into gold at the iris edge like thinning flames around a sun. It was the instant that the disc of cornea had been severed and he had begun to lift, and he realized that he had no recollection of the incision he had just made. For the first time since . . . he could remember since when if he thought about it: since his first cow's eye at State, when Prof. Booke's cold kibitzing had made him slice unsure and send the lens skittering along the counter top . . . for the first time since then, he had let his mind wander when he had an eye under the knife. He had just begun to turn the trepan when his heart took two off-tempo beats and he thought, what would happen if my heart went now, or when I had the old disc out and hadn't got the graft in yet? His mind presented him with a scene out of a Sennett film, he faltering back with his hand on his uniform pocket and careening into a nurse's arms, the trepan landing like a mumbledy peg upright in the cork floor.

It was a routine keratoplasty and the cut was flawless. The woman would see. It wasn't that.

It was that he could not remember turning the instrument, could not now remember it any more than he could remember sugaring his coffee this morning, which he had also certainly done. He could remember placing the trepan and the fractious, insistent rapping of his heart, the remarkable orange sunburst tapering into yellow, and then he could remember that he had begun to lift. But he couldn't remember anything between except the one instant of slapstick vision.

It was what a surgeon always feared of age, that his faculties would scatter and he would no longer be capable of the attention surgery exacted, in which his personal self and present time continued a superficial dumbshow while the essential he passed over a threshold of concentration and, for the requisite ten minutes or two hours or twenty, *became* concentration. He had seen it unimpaired by drunkenness, anguish, anger and physical fear, this ability; but it always, always went with age. It usually did not by God go with age at the age of fifty, and now it was as if Trippin had managed to give him the whole caboodle, not only the promise of an early death but the prelude as well, senility at half a hundred. His memory would be going, he'd be napping in his office next.

He moved heavy and fretful in the narrow cab seat; he couldn't see much point in a compact taxi. Dissatisfied with himself and anxious not to get home for lunch in this frame of mind, he picked the paper up and read the whole article through again, making rude noises so that the driver cocked an eyebrow at him in the mirror. Simply amazing what they could do with facts. Real bullshit. He thought he would give

Hilary a hard time tonight on the subject of journalistic integrity.

But when he glanced back up and saw the by-line his thoughts came to a perplexed halt and he felt wounded, the thing took on another aspect altogether. Andrew Dodds. Why ever . . .?

He told the driver to go back into the centre of town, and he picked up a few other papers at the out-of-state stand. He read all of them on the way home. His words, his statistics, incidents of his past turned over before him in fantastic patterns, ordinary chips of glass in a kaleidoscope. He found it very interesting how the smaller papers printed the Dodds-I.P. story itself and the bigger ones picked their own angle, Washington playing up the security business and Baltimore the sanctity of the human body. He, Rugg, evidently, had never thought about the sanctity of the human body. His picture came in all sizes from half a column to full-page on one of the tabloids; he really ought to get Maeve a photographer's commission for it. If they kept all of it, it would take up pages and pages in the publicity album Maeve kept, though that was already months in arrears and God knew when she'd get them pasted in. He saw certain pages of it: himself in uniform, in the voluminous black silk getup of his honorary degree, with his foot on the shovel breaking ground at Eye Institute in Maine. It occurred to him that of all the newspaper publicity he'd had, none of it had ever had any effect or ultimate significance except as a page of Maeve's scrapbook. He glanced sideward at the widening lawns of the residential section they were entering now, rolling evenly towards the older and more graceful part, white pillars on the houses and the hedges trimmed square along the walks. His face flowed over these in the window, the aggressive nose and chin and brow all just the same as yesterday in the side of the phone booth. He thought, I haven't got used to that yet, I haven't really got hold of yesterday. I'm sorry, but this new thing will have to wait.

But he had a vague sense that this kind of thing didn't wait. When they turned on to his street he felt its presence already there before him, brooding down out of the open windows, waiting in the hot air. You couldn't say a crowd, but everybody out who could be out in the middle of the day, people on their porches chatting, very casual, with neighbours from a few blocks away; and too many dull-coloured cars on the street, clustered towards his house.

"Go right into the drive and around the back," he said, and as the driver turned in Rugg saw another taxi close behind them. They pulled up by the Packard and Rugg paid hurriedly, flushing with anger to see that the other car had followed. He steeled himself to be savage and charged out on to the lawn, but when the door of the second cab opened it was Jadeen who tumbled out, running over the grass to him and catching at the hand he held out towards her, her eyes enormous and ready to spill, grasping his wrist in both her hands and hiding her face against it, "I . . . I felt responsible because I said the same thing."

Her bright hair poured forward over his arm and he stood watching the sun scatter in its colours and amazed, that while his own mind stayed nine-tenths in unfinished business and gave only gradual, grudging place to so much as the material reality of Dodds's outrage; here was Jadeen having accepted it and got half-way across town in a taxicab with it, ready with tears over it and already knowing how she felt about it: responsible!

"Run on in, Jadeen, I'll get your cab," he said. He paid the second fare and followed after her, pausing on the screen porch steps as the two taxis backed out into the gossipy street. He knew that he must hurry, that it must be he and not Jadeen who explained this to Maeve, but he did not know how to compose himself and gather the necessary concentration. He mustn't make a joke of it; that would upset her. Even when, inside, he heard the honking of snarled cars in the street, it did not occur to him that Maeve might not need explaining to. This did not occur to him until he found her in the dining-room, setting the best cups and linen napkins as for a party, panic in her eyes and under them where the muscles pulled the cheek skin taut, but her mouth drawn determined, even a little prim; saying briskly to Jadeen, "Run and get us some lemon, will you, love?" and to Angus, "I made some tea. All the interview offers are on your desk; the *Pittsburgh Weekly* is high bid with twenty thousand dollars, but I finally got sick of it and left the phone off the hook, I hope that's all right. I'm low on tea so I just thought the reporters could wait in their cars. You want some ginger snaps?"

The doorbell began to ring. Maeve cocked her head at him, pert, to be admired. He admired her enormously and he did not know how to tell her that this was no help to him; that he needed her not to minimize it for him but to underline it for him, to . . . what? Not weep, which always made him helpless and only helpless, but to hold him at arm's length, perhaps, to give him the other prim look, the economy-prim instead of the courageous-prim look the way she did when he was about to buy something without a function; to say, "Angus Rugg, now think. Now think about this!"

He dropped the papers on the table and kissed her not any less perfunctorily than usual, slapped her rump for approval and said, "Nothing I could do with like a ginger snap."

187

"And ginger snaps," Maeve called to Jadeen. "In one of the bags on the sink."

The second ring of the doorbell hadn't stopped. Someone was leaning on it, somebody else who had had more time than he to grasp what was happening to him, and had already impudently assumed that he wasn't going to answer. The noise didn't bother him but this impudence did. Maeve moved jerkily setting the table, and it seemed to him that some gesture was expected of him. He hurried down the hall and flung the door open on a half-dozen reporters lustrous and groggy from having waited in the sun, all wearing an identical expression of eager goodwill that, because it was not perfectly successful, looked like something else altogether: dogs panting, or pointing at the kill. Rugg struck a pose and dumped his loudest lecture voice on them, loud enough for Maeve to hear, and Jadeen all the way in the kitchen, "Although I have no statement to make to the press at this time, I think I can safely say that this matter may be regarded with caw-shis optimi-zum." Then he shoved the door shut, locked it, and pulled the wires of the bell mechanism.

But not before a flashbulb had caught him full in the face, producing a painful spot that travelled with his focus. At the table the spot appeared as an orange sunburst on Maeve's forehead, on her swollen abdomen, on the flawed pear on his plate, on Jadeen's slightly heaving pear-plump breast. Their bravado faltered. Maeve kept adding lunch in any order to the table: cheese and chocolates, bread and grapes, liverwurst. Jadeen had to try too hard, she looked from one to the other to make sure of their mood, saying with indignation, "I thought the students were razzing me. Well, I just couldn't believe it!"—which Rugg thought an odd thing for her to pick to say because she had obviously believed it at once. Maeve

188

told a story about Dodi Samson in the supermarket, but Rugg didn't quite get the point of it. The sunburst appeared in Maeve's mouth and he felt that he himself had nothing to contribute: I didn't pay much attention to it at first because I was more interested in my dying.

Jadeen jumped at the slamming of a car door somewhere outside. (Where's Hilary?)

"You-ah *frains* ah with you, hahny," Maeve mimicked Dodi Samson so that Jadeen would laugh. Obedient and eager, Jadeen did so, but he saw Maeve bite the inside of her lip, regretting that she had said the phrase aloud. If the Samsons were their friends who were their enemies and who was against them? Rugg made the effort to smile for her, not jarred as Maeve was by the notion of enmity and opposition, but offended to the core by his "friends'" acceptance and assumption of catastrophe. Was Trippin clucking and rapping his pencil in sympathy by now? Miss Stimpson indignant and defensive? Mama Lily brewing a *bouillon* of protective herbs? Jadeen is sitting in the same chair where she ate her last square meal, but now she has lost her appetite, in commiseration, for my sake. I thank her, but please let's stop for an instant and soberly consider whether anything of significance can happen to a man without his making the slightest contribution to it.

"Going down the hall between first and second periods, even," Jadeen said, "I had the funniest feeling the kids were looking at me. I went and checked to see if my slip was showing, honestly!"

Where there are earthquakes, don't people amuse themselves for weeks, describing what trivial tasks they were engaged in when the trembling started? But this is no earthquake: no fissures, no broken windows, no light poles down.

189

Has anything really happened? We had boiled crab and corn on the cob. I got up and drove to the Chambers, hitting every red light on McPhay. I felt shaky and confused but it left me as soon as I began to talk; the whole thing was vivid in my mind and I felt that I told it well, even brilliantly. I walked in the Quarter for a while, came home, took a pill and went to bed. And somewhere while I slept Andrew Dodds whose eyes I'm trying to save sat up and wrote a story for the International Press. A gloss of my lecture, an interpretation, a critique. Does no one question the relevance of this to me? I've done nothing and said nothing I haven't done and said for twenty years; surely I can't be called to account for Dodds's *metaphor* of it?

". . . when Susan Levy brought the paper in. Susan Levy, her father has the chain of laundromats?" Jadeen went over her story, elaborating it, embedding it in facts. The girl who brought the paper in is the daughter of a laundromat tycoon. Nothing could be more actual than that.

"I asked her what was so interesting . . ."

Footsteps crunched in the drive and Jadeen's voice, all the sounds at the table hung suspended. Maeve lay down her napkin and Jadeen wiped her chin with hers, but they didn't go to see because if it were Hilary he would come in and if it were not Hilary what would they say? The footsteps went away.

"I asked her what was so, I asked her what . . ." Jadeen said and looked desperately from one to the other of them. "I told him I'd call at noon," she pleaded. "He may be waiting for me."

She kneaded her napkin, her eyes entreated Rugg. I should help, he thought; I'm expected to help, I must go to the den with her and try to get through to Hilary. But before he could

gather the energy to offer (the young won't wait), Jadeen
shoved her plate away, put her head down and gave way to
the tears that she had held for, good girl, twenty minutes now.
Maeve laid her hand on Jadeen's hair and averted her eyes
from Rugg. Cry now, he thought, for once I'll welcome it,
Maeve, goddammit, weep. Why must we take such pains to
pretend that nothing's happened when the fact is that nothing
has? What subject are we avoiding, and keeping our spirits up
for what? I could scoff and dismiss this, Maeve, as having
nothing to do with us, but if you summon so much courage,
you've joined the conspiracy to make it matter.

There had been a few peremptory raps at the front door,
and now there was a loud impatient rat-a-tat like a drumstick
on a snare. Rugg shoved himself back from the table and,
telling Maeve to pour him another cup of tea, went back down
the hall, more heavily this time and this time not certain what
he was going to do when he got there. Maybe he should
answer a few things, anyway tell them the medical journals
where he had published all this stuff before. They were just
doing their jobs, after all, if only they wouldn't look so
damned bloodthirsty about it.

The aspect of the street had changed slightly, a whole convention had gathered on the Burns's stuffy-pillared porch
across the street and, dominating the dull cars, a long black
limousine stood dead in the middle of the street with chrome
pomposities at hub and bumper. The reporters had moved
back and were ranged at the bottom of the steps with their
pencils still poised, most of them, over pages that must surely
be blank, mustn't they? Because what would they have written? "The house is white and in need of paint, there is a creaky
swing on the porch and I am standing in a bed of Mrs. Angus
Rugg's forget-me-nots."

A new man had taken the front rank facing Rugg, a man with a complicated face, undulating in all directions like the planes of a mirage: grey wavy hair, tortuous lines on the forehead, a flourish of upper lip and an intense gaze rippling back and forth through the layers of thick trifocals.

"Dr. Rugg," the man announced. "My name is Deke."

He produced a wallet and snapped it smartly open to a photograph of himself mounted on a yellow card, on which the words "DEPARTMENT" and "STATE" were also prominent, though the rest of the profuse printing was so small you couldn't make it out. The man seemed immensely gratified, which struck Rugg as odd because it was only an indifferent likeness, as little flattering as Rugg's own passport picture.

"*Samuel* Deke," the man said and snapped the wallet closed. He was wearing a dark grey suit with too much wool in it for the weather, whose press looked as invulnerable as granite. His body was thickset and rigid, a Norman pillar for his baroque face.

"You've been expecting me, no doubt," he said and smiled convivially. His body made the swift military lift that accompanies a heel-click though his feet didn't move and made no noise.

Well, no, as a matter of fact, I haven't, Rugg thought, and thought that he should be saying this. But instead he yielded to the subtle pressure of the man Deke's body leaning towards him, the briefcase casually against his shin. He stepped back one step, then turned and said, "My office is this way."

At the threshold he waited and watched Deke take in his office, or as much of it as the undulating gaze encountered between door and desk: the candle sockets with faked tallow drippings and ordinary dimestore bulbs, dark panelling, the barometer face saying FAIR and STORMY but not saying which;

below it on the mantelpiece a ship in a bottle, a clumsy but not an ordinary ship in a bottle, one that had been built, Rugg personally knew, by a skipper in a bunk in a ship in the middle of the sea.

The man went around the desk so that he stood behind it and in front of Rugg's own swivel chair. He gestured what might have been an apology for this—Rugg wasn't sure—and set the phone back on the hook. The phone began to ring. On the desk was Maeve's list of interview offers and the monograph that Rugg had been writing the night before last, four centuries ago. "The relative high instance of failure in the case of injury by burning . . ." The rest of the sentence was in his mind.

Hastily, Deke took the receiver off the hook and cut the connection. He picked up the yellow tablet with Rugg's unfinished monograph and set it crossways on the stack of papers to its left, set these neatly crossways on a stack still farther left, then set his briefcase in the empty space. He swivelled Rugg's chair and raised one eyebrow elaborately, doubtful of its comfort. I'm going to be angry in a minute, Rugg told himself. In a minute I'll be seething and shouting. But the minute did not really seem imminent and he didn't invite it. He watched Deke extracting and sorting typed pages from his briefcase. Deke looked up and smiled again, the smile made not a crescent of his mouth but a punctuation brace combining his eyes and nose and referring them to his chin.

"We've got ourselves in a bit of a mess, haven't we?" he said.

He sat. His face was crumpled and curly from the smile and from, weirdly, what Rugg took to be real concern. He couldn't decide if the "we" was the royal-editorial-governess-we, or if the man himself was involved in some way that would turn

N   193 out to be no less credible than the rest of it. Rugg felt as if he were standing in a bottle, had been remarkably constructed inside a bottle so that he could see clearly on all sides of him but could not touch anything or be touched by anything. In his vacuum he evaluated and remembered Now. He told his friends: his name was Deke, rhymes with leek, he had a smile like a handlebar moustache, and he swivelled his ass in my diagnosing chair. His friends laughed and were outraged and indignant for him.

Rugg wanted to know how the anecdote ended. He moved stiffly in his private space and sat down in the harder chair across from Deke.

"It won't be any surprise to you that I've been up since three a.m. We've had a busy morning over you." He went as far as a chuckle to enlist Rugg's sympathy. Rugg appreciated the technique but, inside his bottle, he was unaffected by it.

"But it's quite possible that you haven't had time to grasp all the repercussions of your action of yesterday."

Quite possible, Rugg thought, and he thought, which action did you have in mind? I paid ten dollars for a useless eye, I paid a visit to a cardiac quack, I annoyed my son severely and I took a short-range look at his girl-friend's tongue.

Yet, disconcertingly, the man did in fact have the look of someone who has waked at three a.m. Bloodshot, and a general air of effort. The nosepiece of his heavy glasses sunk into his flesh. His face was formed in such a way that it was quite plausible to suppose you were seeing it through a concave wall of uneven glass. Deke shifted his weight and adopted a more formal expression.

"Certainly it would be difficult for any private individual, be he ever so learned"—he slightly bowed—"to envision the

194

wider implications of so grave an accusation against the honour of the Allied forces in the last days of the war."

He paused for this to sink in, and, to be fair, Rugg tried to let it. Accusation against the honour of the Allied forces. Accusation, honour, ally, forces. Guillaume de Sevres saw a chance to help humanity behind its back, which is usually where you have to do it anyway. He took it and I helped him. What has that to do with the honour of the Allied forces?

"There is virtually no aspect of foreign relations that does not feel the force of such a blow." Always watching Rugg, Deke turned increasingly official. He took from his briefcase and placed before him a folder on which Rugg's name appeared—Rugg had to lean forward to make sure—in that transparent purple ink they use for stamp pads. ("I was already a rubber stamp!" Rugg told his dinner guests, and everyone gasped and tittered and sighed.)

"The military is alarmed not solely because of the security breach involved, but also because of the laxity implied in wartime discipline, and the damage to our image and prestige."

The voice grew more austere and sounded distantly familiar; or not the voice, perhaps, so much as the cadences of it. Like corporals, restless, improvising, convalescing at Reuzarne. An old midwestern military voice, trained to address megaphones and microphones, not ears.

"The judiciary branch finds itself in gravest embarrassment over war-crime trials now being conducted in several parts of the globe. Our friends abroad . . ."

The voice went on. Rugg seemed to have heard the speech, not the words but the rhythms of it, a hundred times before. At Reuzarne, or where? It was rather like the speech a medical man gives to people he doesn't know and doesn't trust: he

195

talks about caring for humanity because the thing he does care about—the way things work, and altering within known laws—are both too cold and too intimate to admit. That was it, that was what the cadence made him think of: the speech that he would make now if, now, he were required to make a speech.

". . . our enemies behind the iron curtain, and especially those Nazis who still remain underground in the Republic of Germany, will rejoice to see our moral foundations shaken in the eyes of the . . ."

"Excuse me," Rugg interrupted, "but you know, your voice sounds a bit familiar. Did you spend any time in the hospital at Reuzarne?"

"It is not often," Deke wavered briefly over a vowel and his face betrayed one instant of alarm, "not often that a man in middle life has the opportunity of redeeming the mistakes of his youth in one single act of patriotic selflessness."

The "middle life" struck into his mind and lodged there until, delayed, Rugg heard as well, "mistakes of his youth" and he thought, my God, how much surer you are than I that I did wrong, and how much less you care. Mistakes of my youth, mistakes of my youth. My youth, but not de Sevres's. No wild oats there, he knew what he was doing. I was hypnotized by him but I knew that too. We had our orders, and we'd say to each other, "We have our orders." Or we didn't say it, it's the same: we knew what we were doing.

"Patriotic selflessness," Deke repeated and closed his eyes in an intensity of emotion like a swoon. I thought, Rugg said impudently to his friends, that he must have written the speech himself.

To Deke he said, "I wondered because I spent the war at Reuzarne, you know."

". . . public statement that your accusation was an imaginative manifestation of overwork and . . . fatigue."

Deke stopped, leaving that one last word apart like a confession. He opened his eyes and looked attentively at Rugg. He was not an ugly man once you got used to all the twists and turns his muscles took him through. Ears flat to the head like tendrils lying to the leaf. Eyes well spaced and only spoiled by the deep and layered lenses: people *will* not take care of their eyes. Well, you see, Rugg said to his dinner guests, his argument was this, that I'd done a foul and bloody deed in my youth, and I could make amends by saying I didn't. How's that? he asked, and they threw up their hands and tch-tched under their breath. Anxiety, palpable but controlled, appeared on Deke's waiting face, and Rugg added not to everyone but to himself and to a few select among them, here was something stranger, I had a harder time taking it in. The man Deke meant this, felt it, he was anxious and in suspense. I thought how curious it was that I have never understood and would now never have time to understand what moved and motivated a man like Deke. I thought perhaps that was a part of my duty and I'd ignored it. I, Rugg, myself, have always dealt in such small, predictable fragments of the living. I know my formulas and I have technique. I can repair an eye. I can make an audience laugh or listen. But you put me in a bottle with whole human people, death and poverty and dishonour, why, I'm a loss, I don't know beans, I have to fall back on a few bleak platitudes I couldn't prove for you and I haven't even, properly speaking, learned: love exists, men are equal, sight matters.

"We are of course prepared," Deke's tired, persuading voice resumed, "to offer you some compensation for the personal embarrassment your selfless sacrifice will cause."

197

He moved abruptly forward and pulled from his briefcase with one hand, like a rabbit from a hat, a handful of cardboard-bound reports, a series of multi-coloured military file reports, a sheaf of reports on the first of which Rugg could see in a faded familiar (so big that the thumbnail eclipsed an eyeball as he worked on it) hand: *Keratoplastie—Novembre 1944—Guillaume de Sevres*.

"... compliments and sincere goodwill, for it is only with the greatest reluctance and regret that the State Department would yield to the necessity of a public ..."

The bottle broke. Rugg felt it happening and he helped it, he thrashed aside and out of it with such force that the papers flew and the phone receiver went crashing down the side of the desk with a plastic and electric crackle. Deke's glasses fell and Rugg gathered up the briefcase, the reports, the man, pummelled and shuffled them all together, shoved them and beat at them, dropped papers, scooped them up and smashed them into the man all down the hall, stumbling himself, not a neat job; pushed and pounded and thrashed the papers everywhichway and back together in his arms around Deke, whom he thrust and was rid of through the front door, saying, shouting to the wide-eyed sleepy hot-ranged reporters in Maeve's flower-bed, "Here! Ask this man! He knows more about it than I know! Ask him!"

He slammed the door and braced himself against it but the pummelling went on, inside him now, as if he, now, were the bottle and someone else were breaking out, the sunbursts flashing, exploding inside him one after the other and he paralysed, powerless against them because each set off the next and each was larger than the last until the last inhabited his entire self and reached tapering in flames to the very limit of the darkness and, simultaneous with the sound of glass

198

breaking somewhere as a window was shattered by a stone, there appeared in the centre of the sunburst a luminous, lucid and astonished understanding: it's going to be this, this is going to be the thing I don't survive.

Calm came back. Shaky, feeling that without the utmost concentration water would flee from him as from a broken bottle, that he would weep, drool, sweat, urinate, Rugg made his way back down the hall and into the dining-room where they were waiting.

Hilary had come, had just arrived because he still stood at the screen porch door with his hand hard on the handle. He had taken it worse than any of them. He was ashen, blue. His face offered itself as a point of livid pallor, and Rugg drew forward by riveting all his force and attention on it. He knew how precarious his balance was when Hilary dropped his eyes, and he felt the carpet shift and waver with them. As if to help, Hilary made an effort to look up; Rugg saw his own difficulty mirrored in the tension of his son's neck, and was unutterably awed and moved by this. He dared to glance at the others and give them a general smile, wishing that someone would say something, welcome him, offer him his tea. The three of them stood expectant and he could not remember what they were waiting for. Jadeen crushed a red cheese rind. Hilary's knuckles went blue-white on the knob, Maeve's eyes had that bottomless patience that demanded answering. All his life, it seemed, people had been waiting for him, depending on him, and he'd always failed to focus on what exactly it was they wanted. I have nothing to say to you, he thought, except that I love you very much.

He said, "Well, boy, I liked your story the best after all," but Hilary's frozen expression didn't alter; hardened, if anything, like Dodds's face, like stalactites on a cave. Something

199

in Rugg at this, almost exhausted, stirred towards anger and despair. They waited, as if all the audiences he had ever faced had been collected and distilled into six unrelenting eyes. Hilary shifted into Jadeen's line of vision and the two of them quivered, rigid, like magnets straining between repelling and attracting poles. Maeve made a gesture that encompassed and put pressure on her womb. Isolated in the stillness these two small movements, attesting that love and birth were happening here, mocked him and admonished him.

"Who was he? What did he say? What did he want?" burst suddenly from Jadeen and Maeve together. Hilary moved towards Jadeen but she put a hand up, to hush or fend him off.

"Wanted me to recant," Rugg said, mistrustfully relieved, hoping that this was all they expected of him. "Wanted me to say I made it up. I've got a nasty indigestion, I'm afraid. Going up for forty winks."

"What did you tell him?" from Jadeen alone this time, fierce and insisting, the pink tongue caught between her lip and teeth.

"Well, but it's true," Rugg said and shrugged, and turned, but Jadeen darted startlingly up and towards him. She spread her hand out towards his chest, and the barest pressure of her fingers made him falter, held him back and down.

"That's what I mean, that's what I meant!" Hilary followed and tried to touch her, but she twisted away and set her back to him. "That's what I meant, sometimes things are just that simple, aren't they?"

She held him there with her eyes, imploring and insisting. You ask too much of me, he thought, I don't know what you want and I can't help you. I don't know anything but fixing eyes. I'm dying. I exempt myself.

"Things can be just that simple, can't they?"

200

"Oh, simple. Well, simple," Rugg said, and watched how the tip of her tongue turned white, caught hard between her teeth.

"Clear, I guess," he said. "Anyway clear."

Her held breath went from her in a nasal sound like snapping metal. Hilary took her arm but she threw him violently off, the effort flinging her in towards Rugg so that her hair brushed and seemed to lacerate his chin. She raised her face to him, too close; the features swam.

"I know that," she whispered. "I knew that all along, but, God, somebody had to help me too!"

On the blurred periphery, Hilary wheeled and smashed his fist into the table; Maeve was leaning on a chair with both her hands. Rugg tried to draw a breath and for an endless instant could not. He looked with terror at Jadeen and her face flowed into focus, terror in it too, and the opposite of terror: outrageous confirmation; adolescent, profitless, and beautiful beyond belief. She smiled at him with almost conspiratorial sympathy, and reached with her mouth to kiss him on the mouth. His skin, astonished, was brittle as a roasted crust.

Hilary thrashed hysterically through the room. "I'm going back to work! I'm going back to work!" he shouted, as if this were a threat, and then absurdly did not do it, but stood shaking at the door.

Rugg steadied himself on Jadeen's shoulder and, using the pressure to free his face from the tentacles of her hair, he managed to turn away. He knew dimly that he could add whatever it was that was happening here to the list of things he would never understand. But he hadn't time for it. He needed all his wits to know that he could make the stairs.

Maeve

After the children had gone Maeve went about the house checking doors and windows, as for a cloudburst except that when it rained she did not lock them. She felt a little foolish about locking the windows, and about not looking out of them as she did so. Two policemen had arrived, and in Maeve's opinion the people were not so much threatening as spectating anyway, hoping to see something shocking, like people at an auto race. She was not afraid of the crowd but she did not want to be tricked into being afraid by seeing it milling there. And she needed something to do. What she would have liked to do is to have appeared on the porch in her apron, shrew with arms akimbo, and scattered them with her broom like so many chickens. She couldn't really have done that so she locked the doors and the downstairs windows.

It was the noise she principally minded. Upstairs she stopped outside the bedroom and listened, but above the sullen drape-deadened voices she could not hear Angus's breathing. One of the contractions started and she hung on to the doorknob and crouched slightly until it should have passed, careful to let her breath out without any sound because she didn't believe Angus could be asleep yet. Angus always snored.

When the pain went away she crossed into the baby's room and assembled the crib—the wing-nuts were rusty and it seemed to take hours—and made it up with new sheets and, her one foolishness, a weightless yellow English blanket that a

202

baby wouldn't need for more than two weeks out of the year in this hot town. Leaving, she noticed that Angus had brought the eye model in and set it on the window-sill. He had cleaned off the pencil marks and patched the lens more neatly, folded all the parts into each other as they were meant to be so that it was recognizable as a human eye and looked out over the room with a bold unshuttered wakefulness. She did not know when Angus had found time to do this, and it wasn't like him. An odd sort of toy and an odder guardian, Maeve supposed; but she found it obscure and touching, and she found that it didn't look bad here, really. The colours suited.

She went back down into the den and picked up the telephone receiver from where it was hanging down the side of the desk. It gave her an ordinary dialtone and when she dialled for the time of day the usual voice came on and said as usual, "One-seventeen p.m. Hire the handicapped. This is a recording."

Satisfied, Maeve looked in Angus's desk memo and, taking a fresh sheet from his yellow tablet, wrote down Chick and Dodi Samson's number. She wasn't going to call Dodi now, with nothing at all to say, but she wrote the number down as a sign of repentant gratitude, and to keep it before her that here was somebody who had offered friendship if she wanted it. She was glad that she hadn't said anything nasty or sarcastic this morning, because it was always one of her father's principles that nothing should be thrown away that was not positively harmful to lay by; and she had seen him proven right at least once, that rotting old rusty-axled peat wheelbarrow no bigger than a child's toy wagon that her mother had made such a fuss about, but that had saved them when the donkey died.

She thought it had been a strenuous day for a poor little

203

near-born baby (it was a boy; she would call him Angus), and that she would go up and give it a nap by its daddy in a minute. But first she took the yellow sheet and copied on to it, just to have there in case she might want it later: Chick and Dodi Samson, BAyou 7-4111.

Hilary

In the car she stared dumb at the pavement going past the window on her side, her body turned from him and her finger-tips on the window-sill, staring righteousness and accusation into the curb. When she got out it changed: she wheeled around with the sudden fright of real good-bye on her face, but it was too late and this only made him angrier. She would just have liked a romantic parting, wouldn't she, that too! He kicked the accelerator and leapt from her.

He took an old school zipcase out of the trunk and up the steps of the *Watch* and in through the glass doors of the news-room. He walked swiftly in an arc left along the wall and made three-quarters of the distance to his desk before he was generally noticed and the noises began to die, voices first and then machines until all you could hear, which he had never before heard here, was the hum of the Linos in the hall behind. He saw Rourk lurch from his chair and the chair continue to bob and swivel as he and Hilary converged on Hilary's desk.

"Hello, Rugg, honey," Rourk said.

Hilary tore the zipcase open and then his middle desk drawer, taking his aspirin box and a spare pair of glasses and two ballpoints that said *Swaggerman Drugs* on them. That was all there was. He'd thought the drawer was full of his stuff but now he looked it all belonged to the *Watch*, the style book thumbed to tatters and the pencils as thick as your thumb, type eraser, copy paper, clips, tacks, art gum, ribbon. He closed the drawer and opened the side top one. Nothing of his in it except a snapshot of Jadeen. Humiliation made him slam it and wrench the bottom one open hard.

"The Deke fellow," Rourk said quietly, "got tossed out, so he evidently asked him to recant. And then what? Was he furious? Frightened? How did he look? What did he say?"

"Oh, for chrissake, Rourk!" Hilary blurted into the silence. "He's got indigestion. Gas pains. What do you want of me?"

Rourk pinched his finger-tips and nodded soothingly. "Indigestion. I think maybe indigestion will do for a start. Did he ask his wife for help? Did he, for instance, lean on her?"

"No! No, he didn't," Hilary said. He sat down slowly, pressing his knuckles on the desk. "He leaned on somebody else. A friend of the family. A girl."

Rourk slid gingerly between the desks and waved Jorgenson out of his chair. He drew it up beside Hilary and slid the drawer shut, out of his way.

"A friend of the family," he said mildly. "Tell me about that."

Jadeen

She was late again but they were only talking at middle volume. It was hotter than yesterday: the smell of their sweat hung around her as familiar as the smell of her own sweat. Two girls at the back had their *Hamlets* open in the aisle between them; Stuart Bordle's hand shot up as soon as she got in the room. She nodded to him to put the hand down and hung her bag on the back of the chair. She swivelled it a couple of times and, staying where she was behind the desk and standing, she said, "Today, I would like to outline for you the theme, or what is called in drama the 'spine', of Shakespeare's *Hamlet*."

She opened her text and smoothed the crevice between the title page and an offset reproduction of Rockwell Kent's ungainly Dane, the style of art that Hilary called "'Thirties Aztec"; she would be calling things by the names Hilary had given them for a long time to come.

Jadeen said, "Thoughts are complex. Actions are not. That is the subject of tragedy. In this sense, *Hamlet* is the prototype of tragedy."

She had lost them. Stuart's feet came crossed out into the aisle; Mary Ellen Church took up her pencil and began to write a note. Something as subtle and solid as window glass slammed shut between them, noise without meaning began and gained momentum. They receded from her as palpably as people outside the window of a starting train, her students that were not really hers but that she knew how to talk to because they came from homes like her home had been on one side or another of the river. And in a mist not luminous like a bayou mist but grey through and heavy with wet, Miss Honeywell receded as well and Cassie Van Looy and Mommy. And Hilary fastest, not even waiting to say good-bye; and Maeve, and Daniel Collins and, strangely, Albert and Miles and all the Negroes she had ever known to call by name. And Angus too. Funny. Angus too.

Ghent, 1965

www.ingramcontent.com/pod-product-compliance
Lightning Source LLC
Chambersburg PA
CBHW031954170626
46807CB00006B/2483